W9-AYP-591

AN AVALON ROMANCE

LEGAL WEAPON
Kim O'Brien

Kate Withers has enough on her plate as the divorced single mother of a nine-year-old daughter with a riding academy to run and an ongoing feud with an unreasonable neighbor. Not to mention the fact that she has never told her ex-husband about their daughter. So when Harry Bond, her ex-husband's brother and lawyer, shows up on her doorstep, she knows things have just gone from bad to worse.

Harry has problems of his own, as it has just been discovered that the divorce he set up for his brother and Kate was never in effect, threatening a family scandal and professional embarrassment. All he needs is for Kate to sign the new papers, and this can all go away. Then he meets her hitherto undisclosed daughter. This new development seems to guarantee a family scandal and severely complicates the divorce problem. On top of all this, Harry finds himself entangled in a legal problem with Kate's academy, and surprisingly attracted to the root of all his current problems, Kate herself.

Thrown together by unpleasant circumstances, an unexpected bond grows between them. Should Kate and Harry give in to this unforseen entanglement of the heart?

LEGAL WEAPON

•

Kim O'Brien

AVALON BOOKS
NEW YORK

PRINTED IN THE UNITED STATES OF AMERICA
ON ACID-FREE PAPER
BY HADDON CRAFTSMEN, BLOOMSBURG, PENNSYLVANIA

I could not have written this book without the invaluable assistance of Debbie Banta, Deb Lyons, Kathleen Y'Barbo, Suzanne Bazemore, Dede Ducharme, Sonja Borstner, and everyone at Avalon Publishing, especially my editors Mira Park and Erin Cartwright-Niumata. Attorneys Nancy Shaw Olvera and Michael Olvera provided a wealth of legal information—any mistakes interpreting the law in this book are my own. I'd like to thank my husband, Michael, for his love and unwavering faith in me from day one, and my children, Beth and Maggie, for their love and support. Above all, I thank the Lord for giving me the inspiration, determination, and persistence to pull this story together.

50122

Chapter One

The Shetland pony jumped the post and rail fence and landed on the rolling, green hills of Crown Oak's golf course.

In hot pursuit, Kate Withers raced after the pony. Her jeans snagged on the same fence the pony cleared, and she thought someone called her name, but she kept going. If Simon realized that Houdini had escaped onto the fairway . . . she didn't want to finish the thought.

Luckily, she saw the pony standing on the putting green of the fourth hole, searching the ground for choice bits of grass.

Hand extended, Kate approached the Shetland. "Houdini," she said softly, and reached in her pocket for a carrot stub. She felt herself relax as he extended his neck toward the carrot. However, before her fingers could close around his halter, a golf ball arced through the air and smacked Houdini's well-rounded rear end.

1

The startled pony shot forward, galloping past Kate, who charged after him.

Joining the chase, two men in golf carts sped past her. They were only making things worse, she knew, fueling the pony's panic. She ran faster, knowing if the carts didn't back off, the pony might hurt itself or someone else. Another cart joined the pursuit, herding the frightened animal down the fairway. Kate's heart pounded even harder when she saw the building in the distance. *Are they crazy?* They were heading straight for the club's concession area, where a number of golfers sat beneath colorful umbrellas eating their lunch.

She shouted a warning which the men either didn't hear or chose to ignore.

Helplessly, she watched the distance between Houdini and the concession area shorten, and the mass exodus begin as the diners became aware of the pony bearing down on them.

Seconds later, Houdini charged right through the eating area, dodging between tables and leaping fallen chairs. People knocked into each other as the confused pony changed directions. Someone screamed. A waiter dove for cover, sending a tray full of salad exploding through the air.

And then two men deliberately overturned their table and toppled the sail of their umbrella right in front of Houdini. As the pony stopped and snorted at this colorful new enemy, the pursuing golfers took advantage of his confusion and surrounded him.

Elbowing past them, Kate reached the pony. Whistling softly, she pulled a carrot stub out of her pocket and extended her hand. The pony swung its head around, recognized her and visibly relaxed. She caught hold of its halter and brushed the long thick forelock out of its eyes. "Oh Houdini. You really did it this time."

The pony crunched the carrot and sniffed her hand hopefully.

"As in the *late* Houdini," a man's voice boomed. "I'm going to kill that pony."

Her shoulders stiffened at the sound of the club owner's voice. *Great. Just my luck. Simon has seen everything.* One look at his tomato-red face told her there was more of a possibility of him having a heart attack on the spot than there was of him forgiving Houdini's misadventure. "I'll pay for all damages."

"You people deserve to be shut down," Simon said.

"Simon, it was an accident." She kept her voice low and soothing, the way she did with frightened horses.

"First, your turkeys roost on my greens." Simon's voice rose. "Second, your dog stalks golfers, and now your pony has demolished my clubhouse." He paused. "There's no judge in the universe that's going to allow your business to stay open."

Simon smiled, but his eyes glittered with malice. "Go down easy, Kate, and maybe I'll leave you enough money for your parents to go to an old folks' home."

"Her parents aren't going anywhere," a man's voice said. "Put down the golf club."

Kate's head swung around at the sound of the voice. She turned and felt the blood rush to her face in a surge so powerful, it hurt. "Harry?" Her voice sounded tinny, incredulous. She cleared her throat and tried again. "Harry Bond?"

She couldn't believe it but the man stepping forward was none other than her former brother-in-law. What was he doing there? He was supposed to be in Boston, running the family law firm. Was she dreaming or had he just handed Simon his business card?

Simon read the card and laughed. "You're a lawyer?" He looked at Kate and snorted. "I bet someone else is suing you." He jerked his thumb in her direction. "Of course, they'll have to wait their turn."

Harry frowned. "I hope Miss Withers didn't injure anything besides her pants on your premises, because *you* would be liable."

Kate's hand whipped around to the back of her jeans and found the flap of what used to be her back pocket.

"Ambulance chaser," Simon stated flatly. He crumpled the card in disgust. However, he noted Harry's custom-fitted white shirt, Rolex on his wrist, and Cole Haan loafers. "It's going to take more than a pretty boy to save you, Kate," he said and stalked off.

When Simon was out of earshot, Kate lifted her chin. "Thank you, Harry, but what in the world are you doing here?" She swallowed and continued to stare at him, suddenly realizing something bad must have happened to her ex-husband. "Is everything . . . well, is Roddy okay?"

"Roddy's fine." Harry stroked the pony's neck but jerked away when the pony bared its teeth and aimed for the buttons on his shirt.

She pulled the pony's head back just in time and tightened her grip on the lead rope. "Sorry, but he's got this thing about Bonds, I mean, buttons."

Harry stared at the pony for a long time before answering. "Roddy is getting remarried."

Her jaw dropped. Roddy was getting remarried? Who would be dumb enough to marry Roddy? But then she remembered nearly eleven years ago, she'd been just that person.

Her lips tightened. "You aren't here to give me a personal invitation, are you?"

Shaking his head, Harry pushed his glasses higher on his nose. "I'm here because your lawyer failed to file the correct paperwork. Legally, you're still married to my brother."

Kate froze in shock. She searched his expression in the hope that he was only joking. "I'm still married to him?"

Harry chuckled and touched her arm. "Don't worry. I've got the new paperwork in the Expedition."

"You're kidding, right?" Kate picked up the pace. Of course she was divorced. Uncle Jeb had done the paperwork himself.

"Would I joke about something so serious?" Harry covered the ground in long, easy strides as the pony jogged to keep up.

No, Kate realized, he wouldn't. She bit her lip and tried to come to grips with her new torrent of emotions. *Uncle Jeb has messed up the divorce? Impossible.*

Yet Harry wouldn't be here otherwise. Roddy always called Harry when he needed someone to bail him out of trouble, do something Roddy considered unpleasant, or solve a problem Roddy couldn't. A mistake in the divorce certainly met all three of those criteria.

Kate led the pony into the barn. Her eyes blinked in the comparative darkness as she walked toward Houdini's stall. "This doesn't make sense," she said. "I have papers."

But do I? She looked away so Harry wouldn't see

the doubt in her eyes. She'd always assumed her uncle had kept the final documents in his office in order to spare her the pain of seeing the proof of the failure of her marriage.

"So does Roddy," Harry said. "However, there's no judge on record by the name of James Kirk. In short, your uncle must have forged them."

Great, Kate thought bitterly, *just great*. She had Simon battling to close down their stable, Harry accusing her uncle of forgery, and now her divorce wasn't final?

"Uncle Jeb forged the papers?" Kate shot Harry a sideways look. "No way."

Jeb might be old but he was completely honest. Besides, he was her uncle and would never do anything to hurt her. Could this be some kind of rotten trick? She led the pony into its stall and latched the door shut behind him.

"It's the truth," Harry insisted. "But don't worry, the agreement I've brought is almost exactly the same. All you need to do is sign it, and I'll be on my way."

"Look, I really think I should call Uncle Jeb." She didn't trust Roddy's brother—even if there was a nagging feeling that he could be telling the truth. "We can call from the stable office."

"Fine." Harry followed her through the stable aisle. About twenty-five horses stuck their heads over their stall doors and watched them pass. "All I want to do is get this signed so I can get out of here."

Kate walked faster. She couldn't get rid of him soon enough.

Chapter Two

A tall blond policewoman looked up from behind a battered metal desk as Harry followed Kate inside the stable office. She was talking on a telephone so old that it actually had a round dial on its face. He stared at a manual typewriter. *Haven't these people heard of touch phones or computers?*

"Maureen," Kate said as she crossed the room. "We need to call Jeb right away."

The blond hung up the phone and looked at him. She seemed vaguely familiar but he couldn't quite place her.

"As I live and breathe," the woman said, "it's Harry Bond."

"Harry," Kate said, "you remember Maureen Reilly, don't you?"

"It's Officer Reilly to you," the blond informed him.

Suddenly it clicked and he remembered her from Roddy's wedding. She'd ticketed his brother for illegally parking outside the church, and for having a broken tail light. He'd paid the fine, of course.

"Nice to see you again, Maureen," Harry said. "You're looking well. Still a policewoman I see."

Maureen gave a short, curt nod. "Still defending your numbhead brother?"

"Maureen!" Kate said.

Harry ignored the insult to Roddy. He hadn't driven more than three hundred miles to argue his brother's intellectual abilities. He'd come to avoid a family scandal. He could care less what Maureen Reilly thought about his brother.

"There's a problem with the divorce papers," Kate admitted. "Harry thinks Jeb messed up."

"Impossible," Maureen said. "I witnessed the document myself."

Harry shrugged. "If you don't believe me, just look at the so-called official seal. It could have come out of a cereal box." He ran his fingers through his short hair. "I can't believe no one noticed until now."

"Kate's been busy," Maureen snapped. "Responsibility does that to a person." She glared at him. "Of course none of *you* people give a darn about that."

"Maureen." Kate's voice was full of a quiet warning that Harry didn't fully understand.

"What?" Maureen said. "What's the matter? It's the truth." She studied Kate and then asked, "What happened to your jeans?"

"It's a long story." When Maureen continued to stare at her, she added, "I tore them on Simon's fence. Houdini got loose on the golf course."

"Wonderful," Maureen stated. "The judge is going to love this." She shook her head. "Of course, Simon will add this to the lawsuit. That pea-brain Simon probably let the pony out himself."

Lawsuit? Harry felt the knee-jerk impulse to ask,

reminded himself it was none of his business, and kept his lips firmly sealed. New papers signed, home by 11 o'clock. That was the plan.

Maureen handed her a colorful scarf from her pocket. "Here, stuff that in your pocket. It'll cover the tear. I'll go ticket that sleazebag for a broken tail light."

"He doesn't have a broken tail light," said Kate, who took the fabric.

"He will when I'm finished with him."

"You can't do that."

"Of course I can. I'm hell with a slingshot."

Broken tail light? The gleam in Maureen's eye reminded him of what'd happened to Roddy's car at the church.

"You can't," Kate repeated. "Someone will see you and report you. We don't need any more trouble."

She glanced over her shoulder at the damaged back pocket. Following her gaze, Harry's thoughts couldn't help but return to the image of her charging across the golf course with the flash of pink peaking out of the torn back pocket of her jeans. When he'd seen her charging across the golf course, he'd instinctively joined the chase. Not because he wanted to help her, but because there had been no one else who would.

He had the same feeling now that Kate was in over her head with problems and no help was in sight. With effort, Harry summoned up his most professional stance. "Get your lawyer on the phone. I haven't got all day."

The words had hardly left his mouth when the door to the office banged open and a girl stepped inside. She had a head full of thick, dark curls. As she swaggered over, he noticed her eyebrows rising like dark wings above almond-shaped eyes. Funny, those eyes looked just liked Roddy's.

Harry stared at the heart-shaped freckle slightly to the left of her mouth. Roddy had a birthmark like that in just the same place. He had one as well. It ran in their family.

For the first time Harry could remember, words simply failed him. Part of his brain whirled in high speed as it tried to come up for another explanation for the reason this girl had Roddy's wild hair, and eyes the color of pencil lead.

"Hey Mom, Gramma sent me to get you for dinner," the girl said.

A huge calico-colored cat leaped onto the well-worn leather sofa. The whooshing noise of the air deflating from the cushions could have come from his lungs. He didn't need to do the math.

This explains everything, he thought. *No wonder Kate is so eager to get rid of me. It is all part of the coverup.*

He watched the color drain from Kate's face, which surely signaled guilt. He crossed his arms and waited.

"Hey Aunt Maureen," the girl said. "You going to teach me some more self-defense moves today?"

Maureen shook her head. "Not today peanut." She stepped closer to Kate, who was staring at him with a strangely intense expression on her face.

Then the girl looked at him. "Hello."

Kate's chin lifted a fraction. "This is my daughter Jane," she said. She put her arm over her daughter's shoulder. "Jane, this is your Uncle Harry."

Harry shook the slender hand that disappeared easily within his own. *This is my niece?* What would Roddy say when he learned about his daughter? Not to mention what it would do to his mother. They'd sent him down here to avoid a scandal. He never dreamed he'd uncover one.

"Wow," Jane said. Her eyes opened wide in wonder. "Uncle Harry?"

"Pleased to meet you, Jane." Harry deliberately spoke her name slowly, letting his voice seal the bond that already existed by virtue of their blood.

This changes everything, he thought. If Kate thought that he would let Roddy sign any kind of divorce agreement without adding a custody arrangement, she was crazy. No way would he walk away from his brother's child. His niece. The words nearly blew his mind. The lawyer in him wanted the details: The date of her birth, blood tests to confirm the DNA, a copy of the birth certificate. Yet, deep inside, he knew these documents would only confirm what his eyes and heart already knew. Roddy had a daughter that Kate had kept a secret for years. Harry was an uncle—and this uncle wasn't leaving until he got everything straightened out.

"Is Uncle Harry having dinner with us too?" Jane asked.

"No," Kate said, at the same time Harry replied, "Yes."

Chapter Three

Roddy hadn't told anyone about Jane. What a surprise. Kate wanted to shake her ex-husband until his teeth fell out. No one could fake the kind of surprise she'd seen in Harry's eyes. No one could question Jane's resemblance to Roddy, either.

On the path ahead of her, Jane and Harry walked together so closely their sides nearly touched. Her daughter's head tilted toward her uncle's voice, reminding Kate of a flower straining for the sun.

For so long she'd wanted Roddy and his family to acknowledge Jane, but now that they had, well, would Roddy show interest in Jane, or would it end only in more heartache for her daughter? More than anything, she wished she could spare Jane the pain she herself had experienced, and felt a renewed determination to protect her daughter.

The thoughts continued to swirl in her mind as they approached the old Victorian house. Tall and latticed, it reminded Kate of a grand old dame who had aged with grace and dignity. She stared at the purple front door, and fought the urge to grab Jane, run inside, and lock Harry outside.

Her leather paddock boots had barely touched the front step when the door opened, followed by the bang of the screen door, which had slipped off its springs again.

"Harry? Harry Bond?" Her mother's voice boomed as if Harry stood at the foot of the hill instead of a few feet from her door. "Is that really you?"

Her mother extended her hand in greeting. Arthritis had spread like wildfire through her mother's hands, burning away the strength in her hands, and leaving swollen red knots in the knuckles.

Kate let her breath out slowly as Harry took her mother's hand, clasping it as carefully as if it were a small bird given into his care.

"Mrs. Withers, hello."

Kate watched his gaze sweep over her mother, smiling as he looked at her mom's favorite blue sweatsuit with its grinning horse and words proclaiming her mother a Barn Beauty.

"It's Prissy, remember? Mrs. Withers is much too formal." She turned to Kate. "Is everything okay? Roddy didn't up and die, did he?"

Kate sighed. "Of course not Mom, but it's a long story."

Her mother's gaze returned to Harry. "You've met Jane, I see. Isn't she a sweetie?"

"Grandma," Jane protested.

"She certainly is," Harry agreed. He gave Kate a pointed look. "Meeting her was quite a surprise."

Kate set her jaw. She knew he thought she'd purposely kept her daughter a secret from his family. Let him think what he wanted. She refused to discuss Roddy in front of Jane.

"Well," Kate's mom said in the uncomfortable silence between them. "Some surprises are good ones." She smiled from Kate to Harry. "Like you showing up on our door step after all these years."

Inwardly, Kate groaned at the speculation in her mother's expression. Her parents always had had a soft spot where Harry was concerned. Even at her rehearsal dinner before the wedding, she recalled Prissy urging her to dance with Harry.

"You'll join us for supper, won't you Harry?" Before he could reply she added, "It's lamb stew."

"I'd be delighted," Harry said. "Provided that I get to sit next to Jane."

Jane beamed. Kate's hands clenched into fists. She wanted to warn her daughter not to get attached to Harry. A man like him knew all the right words to say. But in the end, Harry would do as he pleased, regardless of the hurt he would leave behind.

Kate's mom pulled the door open wider. "Come on in before the Guinea hens see you and start making a racket. Simon will call the police again."

Knowing Harry wasn't exactly an animal person, Kate felt compelled to explain. "Guinea hens are sort of like wild turkeys, but smaller." She hesitated. "A bit more noisy too."

Harry smiled, but the expression faded abruptly when a chorus of prehistoric-sounding screams echoed from the surrounding pine trees.

"Those are the Guinea hens," Kate explained.

"They don't eat people, do they?" Harry asked.

Her mother whooped with laughter. "Of course not. If they did, we wouldn't be having this little problem with Simon."

This "little problem" was a court injunction against

their business prohibiting them from giving riding lessons. Simon had initiated the charges about a month ago after one of his golfers had driven into the water hazard because two Guinea hens had chased him away from their nest. There were other charges as well, and now with Houdini's latest escapade, the court might very well order them closed permanently.

"Harry's here on business," Kate said. She searched for a way to soften what needed to be said about her divorce agreement.

Her mother released her breath as if the answer was obvious to everyone but Kate. "Of course he is." She smiled at Harry. "We knew you'd come as soon as you heard about our legal problems."

Harry shifted his weight from foot to foot. "Actually," he began, but stopped as Georgie, the Newfoundland mix, jumped up on him and slapped a huge, wet kiss on his lips.

"Harlan is not going to believe this." Kate's mother clasped her hands together as Harry wiped his mouth. "This is a true miracle." She gestured them into the hallway. "Harlan's practicing our opening defense statement. It contains the entire history of our stable."

"Oh no," Kate groaned. "If Dad reads everything he's written, he's going to put everyone to sleep."

"Exactly," her mother nodded emphatically. "It's all part of his strategy. He's hoping they'll dismiss the case just to shut him up." She shot Harry a measuring glance. "Of course all this is going to change now Harry's here."

A man's voice drifted into the hallway, ". . . and that concludes March nineteen-sixty-one. Now we'll turn to April. The first was an unusually cold day . . ."

"Harlan, Kate's here." Her mother's voice rang with

pleasure. "You aren't going to believe who's with her."

Her dad—a tall, thin man with horn-rimmed glasses and white hair—emerged from the study. He looked at Harry intently, and after a long moment extended his hand. "Been a long time."

"Too long," Harry replied.

"Nine years to be exact," Kate pointed out.

Her mother led Harry to an old, blue sofa. "The point is that he's here now." She beamed down at him. "Harry, how are you?"

Kate watched as the old sofa gave an alarming creak as Harry settled his weight onto it. The down cushions deflated under him, too, sending wisps of cat hair into the air.

Before Harry could reply, Prissy answered for him. "He looks good, doesn't he?"

Considering the shock of discovering his status as an uncle, Kate thought Harry did look pretty good. "Maybe you should bring him some iced tea," she suggested.

"It's good to see you again, Harry," Harlan said. He settled himself into the blue leather recliner that had been his chair for as long as Kate could remember.

"You too, Harlan." Harry shifted on the couch and pushed his glasses higher on his nose. "But I'd better set the record straight. I'm only here because something needs straightening out."

"And it's about time!" Prissy shouted from the kitchen. Although her mother might be close to seventy, her hearing was as sharp as ever. "We always thought Kate married the—"

"Mom," Kate interrupted before her mother could proclaim that her daughter had married the wrong brother. "That's not why Harry's here."

"Roddy's getting married again," Harry said gently. "However, there's a problem with the divorce papers."

"A problem with the divorce papers?" Prissy echoed as she walked back into the room. The ice in the glasses clinked audibly in the silent room as she set the tray on the table.

"They're not legitimate," Harry said.

"Of course they're legitimate."

Harry and Kate exchanged glances. "Uncle Jeb may have made a mistake," Kate said as gently as she could.

"Something very serious was omitted." Harry gave a long and pointed look at Kate.

"I'll explain everything later," Kate said. She gave her mother a look which she hoped her mother understood meant she didn't want to discuss things in front of Jane.

Harry smiled at Jane. "It might take a couple of days to work things out."

Prissy beamed. "Take your time. You'll stay with us, won't you, Harry?"

Harry winked at Jane. "It'd be a pleasure."

"Hurray!" Jane shouted.

Kate wanted to shout, too, but not with pleasure.

"Harry, will you say grace?" Harlan asked as they sat around the kitchen table.

Across from him, Jane clasped her hands together in prayer. Her angelic expression contrasted with the dark wildness of her hair. Harry had bet she gave everybody a run for their money. He nearly smiled. Roddy still had a lot of the devil in him too. Famous for his mad-man style of riding, Roddy seemed unable to live his life any more conservatively than he rode.

Their mother considered Roddy directly responsible for every gray hair on her head.

He realized how quiet the table had become and forced himself back into the present. He hadn't given grace since his father had been alive, but found the old childhood prayer coming back.

"Father we thank you for this meal, for blessings you have given us, and most of all for Your love."

"Amen," everyone said.

With a clink of silverware, and the clatter of dishes, the meal began.

"Have some more stew, Harry," Prissy urged.

As if he needed urging. When was the last time he'd had a home-cooked meal? He couldn't help but remember when he'd gotten the flu and his girlfriend had brought him chicken noodle soup. Not only had she left the dish outside the front door, but also it had tasted exactly like the kind made by the local deli.

"So Jane, how was school today?" Harlan asked.

"Well," Jane stated with the air of someone about to tell an exciting story, "the boys are trying to convince the girls that there's a ghost in the girls' restroom."

As Jane launched into the entire story, complete with waving hands and animated facial expressions, Harry laughed aloud along with the rest of the family. Clearly, she had her father's charm and way of telling a story.

His gaze returned to Kate. He watched the ice jiggle in her glass as her unsteady hand brought the tumbler to her mouth. She looked thin, fragile, and unhappy. Why had she kept Jane a secret all these years? Even more important, did Roddy know about his daughter? Harry had to believe he didn't. Everything in him was dying to ask the question outright, but not now, not here in front of Jane, who stood only to get hurt by the answer. Either her mother had lied for years, or her father had outright rejected her. No. He'd wait until he could get Kate alone and then he'd grill her. He narrowed his gaze, studying his intended witness, memorizing the cast of her eyes, the set of her lips. Being a lawyer had taught him to read people well. If she was lying when he asked why she'd kept Jane from knowing his side of the family, he'd know it.

However, immediately after dinner, Kate pushed back her chair. "Time for bed, Jane."

"Oh Mom, could I please stay up late and talk to Uncle Harry?"

Harry arched his eyebrows and nodded his support of the idea.

Kate shook her head. "It's a school night, muffin."

"But *Mom*. It's Uncle Harry's first night here." Tears shimmered like jewels on the ends of her long, black eyelashes.

"Don't worry," Prissy said, "Harry will be here tomorrow and as long as he wants."

"It's already late," Kate said. "Let's get going."

Harry didn't know whether to be impressed or disappointed when, without a further protest, the girl headed toward the stairs. "See you in the morning," Jane said brightly to Harry, and then skipped away, climbing two steps at a time.

Prissy turned to Harry. "You've had a busy day as well. I've made up the guest room for you."

He gave a curt nod. Oh, he'd stay alright, and tomorrow Kate could explain everything. He'd need to draw up new divorce papers as well. No way would he let Kate get away with what she'd done. He had vacation time coming, and he'd use as much of it as necessary to get to the bottom of things. His brother's child was at stake.

Prissy led him up three flights of stairs to an attic bedroom. He'd stayed there once, right before Roddy's wedding. He remembered the rose-printed wallpaper, and the way the bed nestled between the eaves.

Prissy turned on a light and pointed to the bed. "Sheets are fresh. You'll find towels in the bathroom." She hesitated in the doorway. "Harry?"

"Yeah?"

"I'm really glad you came."

Harry wondered if she would still think so when he left with a new child custody arrangement. "Thanks," he said.

Prissy seemed to want to say something else, so Harry let the silence lengthen between them. "I've always had a good feeling about you," she said at last, "that you weren't the kind of person who could walk away if you saw someone who needed your help." She pushed a thick stack of papers into his hands. "This is the paperwork on the injunction against the riding academy." She backed away slowly. "We're in trouble, Harry. Big trouble."

Immediately after she left, Harry set the file down and pulled out his cell phone. He wanted to throw the receiver out the window when Roddy's answering machine picked up. "Come on, Roddy, I know you're there. Pick up."

He spoke into the answering machine until it disconnected him, hoping Roddy would pick up the phone. He didn't. Frowning, Harry stared at the phone in his hand. Punching in numbers, he left urgent messages for his brother at every place he could think of.

Great, he thought, *just great.* Roddy was probably deliberately avoiding his calls, hiding out somewhere until Harry showed up on his doorstep with the new divorce papers signed and sealed. He felt the familiar frustration that his brother had the guts to jump horses over objects almost as tall as a man, yet ran from facing his ex-wife.

His brain whirled as he settled into the bed and pulled the down comforter over himself. He needed to research New York State legislature for child support and parental rights. The divorce agreement needed amending too. His mother would be shocked to discover herself a grandmother. She'd probably fly to the Arizona spa she favored for an emergency facial toning procedure just to assure herself that she didn't look old enough to be a grandparent.

Harry placed his glasses on the night table on top of the folder Prissy had given him. The hem of the lace curtains lifted as a thick, cool breeze passed through the room. The fall air smelled vaguely spicy and brought back vague memories of Halloween and cold apple cider. The down comforter felt good on his body too. A beam of moonlight illuminated the room just enough for him to make out the shapes of the furniture.

He heard the flush of a toilet, and the sound of a door shutting. Moments later, a child's laughter floated up the stairs and then Kate's voice said good night to her parents and Jane. He lay there listening to the house settle, and then go still.

Sometime later, he felt the foot of the bed depress, as if someone was stealthily climbing onto the mattress. Half convinced it was all a dream, Harry kept his eyes closed. Inch by inch the weight on the mattress moved closer to him, until it pressed warm and heavy against his back.

Harry turned and gazed into a pair of dark eyes glistening in the moonlight. For a moment, he nearly screamed and then recognized the dog. He probably slept in the dog's usual place.

The dog grinned. Its massive head revealed gleaming white teeth and a long, lolling tongue. As if pleased she'd finally awakened him, Georgie poked her nose under his hand. Harry found himself stroking the long, silken coat. "You better not snore," he warned Georgie, who lowered her head onto his pillow.

Harry looked out the window at the stars, and for the first time since he'd arrived, wondered just exactly what he'd gotten himself into.

Chapter Four

The next morning, just before dawn, Kate slipped out of the house and walked down the hill to the barn. After quickly feeding and watering the horses, she headed for the pasture. The dew soaked her paddock boots and hems of her Levi's as she climbed a small hill to the sun-bleached rock where she came every morning.

Lord, what will happen now that Harry knows about Jane? Whatever it is, please don't let Jane be hurt. I can handle anything except that.

The wind swept gracefully through the trees and offered a gentle touch on her cheek but no assurances. The sun slowly lightened the sky, but it, too, failed to illuminate a solution. At the same time, these familiar elements touched something elemental and deep inside Kate. Although she didn't attend church, all she had to do was look at the swell of land, held within the embrace of the sky, to know it had all come from a master plan. Just how that plan would play out, she wished she knew.

How could Jeb have messed things up so badly?
She ran her fingers through her hair and knew her
uncle wasn't entirely at fault. She should have checked
the papers more thoroughly, instead of allowing Jeb
to handle everything. At the time, she hadn't wanted
to hurt his feelings by questioning the process. Another part of her, she admitted, had thought Roddy
would come to his senses and contest the divorce. She
could see now that her mistake could change Jane's
life.

In the distance, she traced the length of fence that
bordered Simon's golf course. According to New York
State law, the old post and rail was six inches below
code. Simon had seized this discrepancy in height as
an opportunity to initiate the lawsuit. To raise the
fence around the entire pasture would cost about
$10,000, money the riding academy just didn't have.

Her gaze fell on an old lean-to, a wooden structure
that had stood for ages unused in the pasture. If she
tore it down, she could use the lumber to raise the
fence height along the stretch nearest the golf course.
The judge would see the stable was trying to meet
code and perhaps lift the injunction.

She curled a strand of hair around her finger
thoughtfully. It was a long shot, but it might just work.
Besides, it would keep her mind off things—like
Harry. He might charm her parents and Jane, but she
wasn't letting her defenses down for an instant. So
what if he was gentle when he shook her mother's
hand, or if he had listened to Jane's stories as if they
were the most interesting ones he'd ever heard. And
forget that he had rushed to her rescue when Houdini
had escaped on the course. *He is a Bond. And that
means trouble in capital letters.*

She hurried to the barn and grabbed a crowbar and sledgehammer off the shelf in the grain room. A quick glance at her watch told her she had about an hour before Jane caught the bus for school.

Hefting the tools over her shoulder, she headed for the old shed where her thoughts immediately returned to Harry. He looked almost exactly the same as the last time she'd seen him nearly ten years ago. He was taller than Roddy, heavier built with a breadth of shoulders a woman's hand would barely span. His hair was lighter in color, too, and straight where Roddy's had curled. And his eyes were hazel, more brown than green. She could just picture him fixing that gaze on some unfortunate witness and not blinking until he got the response he wanted. Or, if it were a woman, maybe he smiled. He looked nice when he smiled at Jane.

Wait a minute. She had to stop thinking about Harry and get back to work. Lifting the sledgehammer, she slammed it against the structure's side. The impact sent shockwaves along her shoulders, down her back and into her legs. The work would be harder than she'd initially thought. She swung the sledgehammer again and the plank loosened.

This one's for Simon, she thought, belting the wood with all the strength she had. *For the lawsuit.* She lifted the sledgehammer again. This one's for Roddy, she thought, *for being such a worm and not telling his family about Jane. But why stop at Simon and Roddy?* She'd swing the sledgehammer for every slimy man who ever walked the earth. With a satisfying thud, the first board clanked to the ground.

Kate wiped her brow and admired the gap in the wall. "Not bad."

"What are you doing?"

Swinging around in disbelief, Kate watched Harry cross the remaining distance between them. He wore the same button-down shirt and trousers as yesterday, but somehow they looked neat and freshly pressed. They probably were, thanks to her mother. She braced herself. "Morning, Harry."

Harry glared at the tool in her hands. "What do you think you're doing with that?"

Kate shifted the hammer to her other hand, nearly dropping it in the process. "I'm tearing down the lean-to."

"Why?"

"For the wood." She rolled her eyes when he continued to stare at her. "To raise the fence."

Harry's gaze swung over the old structure. "Most of it has dried out. You'll crack more boards than you can salvage."

Kate rolled her eyes. Trust a man to always think he knew better. "I don't care how rotten the wood is," she stated. "I'll duct-tape the thing together if I have to."

"Well, you should take off the roof first. If you don't, it could fall on you."

A flicker of unease crossed her mind. It did make sense to bring the roof down first. Working with sledgehammers wasn't exactly her strong suit. She looked at the tool and wondered what else she had overlooked. "Thank you."

"You never were very good with tools," Harry pointed out. "Roddy was always telling me some story about you flooding the basement with the washing machine, or nearly hanging yourself from the ceiling fan."

Kate put her hands on her hips. "I fixed the ceiling

fan," she couldn't resist pointing out. "It wasn't my fault my hair got caught in it."

Harry snorted. "According to him, you were standing on your tiptoes and shouting for help."

"Well maybe if he'd been around more, I wouldn't have had to fix everything myself."

Darn, I didn't intend on letting him goad me into making any remark about Roddy. She lifted her chin a fraction higher. "Just leave if you've come here to make fun of me."

"I came here to find out about my niece." Harry's expression hardened. "Why didn't you tell Roddy about Jane?"

Kate tilted her head to meet his gaze. "What makes you think I didn't?"

"Because he would have mentioned her otherwise."

Kate shrugged. "Would he?"

Harry shoved his glasses higher on his face. "Of course."

"I don't think so, Harry." Kate turned her back to him and eyed the old lean-to critically. "He wanted kids about as much as a tree wants root rot." She raised the sledgehammer shoulder height. "You should leave things alone."

"I'm sure you would like that," Harry stated, "but it isn't going to happen. There'll be a new agreement, of course, when I know what kind of parental rights Roddy wants me to exercise."

Kate spun around. "Fine," she said, "talk to Roddy and you'll discover the only thing he wants to exercise is his horse."

Only after he left did Kate let herself admit how badly he'd shaken her. First the lawsuit, then the divorce problem, and now a possible custody battle over

Jane? She drew a shaky breath and reminded herself that Roddy hated children, and as soon as Harry realized this, he'd be on his way.

Inside the house, Harry asked Prissy for permission to use the phone. Taking one look at his face, she had led him into Harlan's study and closed the door behind him. Harry wasted no time in punching in his brother's home phone number.

As the number rang, he looked around the room at the book shelves filled with trophies of every shape and size. Faded championship ribbons of blue, red and yellow colors dangled from inside some of them. His gaze traveled to the framed photographs on the wall. Most of them showed Kate at various ages on horses of different sizes and colors. He spotted her crouched over the neck of a reddish-brown horse jumping over an enormous stack of thick logs. The plaque on the frame read, UNITED STATES EQUESTRIAN TEAM— GLADSTONE TRIALS.

"Come on, pick up," Harry muttered. When the answering machine came on, Harry left a short, cryptic message and hung up. Next he dialed his brother's cell phone, and then the stable where his brother kept his horses, and left messages there as well.

Harry glanced out the window. Kate had placed a ladder against the lean-to and was in the process of climbing on top. Harry watched her stride across the slanting roof. She didn't even know how to crouch to keep her balance. If she wasn't careful, she'd slip and slide right off the edge.

Hurrying to the back door, he reminded himself it wasn't his responsibility what happened to Kate. Just because he'd suggested taking down the roof first, it wasn't his fault if she fell off it. Yet the thought bugged him, and the guilty feeling spread as he imagined her tumbling off the roof.

Banging the door shut behind him, Harry stopped trying to convince himself of his own innocence. His stride lengthened into a dead run down the path. Why in the world had he ever suggested to someone as bad with tools as Kate, that she take down the roof?

Chapter Five

On the roof, Kate forced herself to focus on the problem at hand—dismantling the lean-to. Where should she begin? In a few places the shingles had fallen off leaving bald patches of brownish-red wood beneath, and this seemed as good a place as any.

Using a crowbar, Kate struggled to pry off a shingle. After several attempts, she cracked it in half, and tossed the pieces over the side of the shed.

"Ouch!"

Ouch? Kate scampered to the edge of the roof and peered over the edge. Oh no. It was *him*. Her heartbeat accelerated. "Harry? What are you doing?"

The man in question stood halfway up the ladder, rubbing his head. "Trying to help you and nearly getting a concussion in the process."

"You want to help me?" Kate repeated. She frowned down at the smudge on his forehead. "Are you okay?"

He adjusted his glasses. "Yeah. I have a hard head."

Knowing he wasn't truly hurt, Kate relaxed slightly.

"It runs in your family." She knelt for a better view. "Well, did you reach Roddy?"

"No," Harry admitted.

"You won't," Kate predicted. "He's never returned any of my phone calls either. He has a sixth sense when it comes to matters about Jane." She struggled to keep the bitterness out of her voice.

"You don't know my brother," Harry argued. He climbed up another rung so he was nearly eye level with her. "And you apparently have a death wish as well. You've defied every law of gravity known to mankind, not to mention nearly lopping off your foot twice with the sledgehammer."

Kate's eyes narrowed. *He's been watching me? How long?* "What I do isn't any of your business, is it?" She backed away from the edge of the roof.

Although she didn't see him, she felt the structure wobble as he climbed onto the roof behind her. "It is when it involves my niece. It's going to be a lot harder to get you to sign anything if you're in intensive care."

Kate shrugged. "I can take care of myself."

She heard him make a noise of frustration. *Good.* Now if he would just leave. She had a lot of work to do.

"Give me the crowbar," Harry ordered. "I'll show you how to it."

He took the tool from her. The crude iron implement, wrapped in his fingers, looked right at home in his grip. Bending, he hooked a slate shingle with the bar. With a quick twist, the small rectangle popped off as easily as if it had been thumb-tacked in place. "See?"

Maybe it was because things looked out of proportion when viewed from a roof-top perspective, but outlined with the trees and sky, Harry seemed larger, radiating strength and an uncomfortable level of masculinity. Kate stared at the opening where his shirt parted to show his chest and neck. Something in her that had been thirsty for a long time couldn't help but be drawn to that pool of skin.

This is Roddy's brother, remember? She stepped backward only to have him grab her arm.

"Kate, be careful. You're on a roof, remember?"

How could she forget? The footing was slanted, slick, and uneven under her feet. However, she was better off taking her chances with it than letting Harry get one step closer. She pulled her arm away, nearly unbalancing them both. "Don't touch me."

"Gladly," Harry said. "I probably shouldn't talk to you either. Now that there's a child involved, all communications between us should go through your attorney."

"Fine," Kate said.

Harry turned his back and hacked away at the roof. Kate tried to imagine Harry and her Uncle Jeb locked in a legal battle. Harry would probably get bossy, which Jeb wouldn't like. If this happened, her uncle probably would turn off his hearing aid the way he did whenever anyone said something he didn't like.

"You can give me the crowbar now," Kate said after a while. "I've got the idea."

Harry kept his back to her, displaying the neat line of his hair against a strong-looking neck. She suspected this strength to be more than physical, and wondered why, just once, someone like Harry couldn't be on her side. Just as quickly, she brushed the thought aside.

"You can give me the crowbar back," Kate repeated.

"In a bit," Harry muttered.

"You don't have to do this."

"Just a sec."

Uncomfortable with watching him work, and with the strange thoughts that played unwanted in her mind, Kate climbed down the ladder and retrieved a second crowbar from the tool shed. Although the shingles didn't pop off the roof as they did for him, she felt a grudging pleasure when Harry gave her an approving nod.

As they worked in silence, Kate couldn't resist sneaking peeks at him. His body silhouetted against the late-September sky looked lean and strong. His face, closed in concentration, offered no insights into his mood or character. As if he felt the weight of her stare, Harry turned to her.

"Be careful, Kate. Without the shingles this structure is even more rickety than I thought."

"The wood's fine." Kate yanked the crowbar under a plank, embarrassed she'd been caught staring. The board gave way with a creaking noise. "We'll have enough to raise the fenceline that parallels Simon's golf course."

Harry frowned. "You're going to have to raise it six inches." He paused at the surprise on her face. "Your mother gave me a copy of the grievance last night."

Kate drew her fingers through her hair and felt her fingers come away damp. "You know about the lawsuit?"

"You can't give lessons because your fence is too short, and your animals escape and endanger golfers," Harry summarized.

"We're the ones in danger from his golfers. They're the worst shots I've ever seen."

Harry's lips twitched. Kate looked away. She'd seen this expression before. Any minute, he would act just like the numerous other lawyers she had seen. He'd smile, wink, and tell her how absurd the whole case was.

"I'm serious," Kate continued. "I can't tell you how many windshields they've broken by their mishits."

"There were other code violations as well," Harry said, straight-faced. "Wiring, hay storage, the presence of farm animals." He cleared his throat. "Specifically, Guinea hens."

Kate sighed. "Our barn is more than a hundred years old. The codes were different then." She heard the frustration in her voice. "The point is that the lawsuit against us is malicious. How can we prove that?"

"Not easily." Harry crouched back on his heels and shielded the sun with his hand.

"Malicious intent," Kate prompted. "If Simon can bankrupt us, he can buy the land from the bank."

"You should concentrate on fixing the items outlined in the summons." A trace of a smile played around the edges of his mouth. "Get rid of the attack chickens." A chuckle rumbled from his chest. "You can't have them pecking the golfers."

Some help he is, Kate thought in disgust. *I should have just kept my mouth shut.*

"Of course you could hire an accountant to put together a reasonable proposition for financing the fence." His hand swept over the stretch of land around them. "This land has to be worth a lot of money. You could use it as collateral."

Kate shook her head. "We're already mortgaged.

We need to win this case. Can't we counter-sue for harassment?"

"Not when it's your pony who's doing the harassing."

Although Kate realized the truth in Harry's assessment, it still frustrated her that he was so quick to take Simon's side. Would it kill him to offer one bit of help? Turning her back, she attacked another shingle with the crowbar.

"You're going to fall over backwards, Kate," Harry said. "If you keep leaning so far back."

There he goes again, telling me what to do. Kate deliberately leaned even farther back. Trusting a sense of balance that had been fine-tuned since birth, she played with gravity as she pulled the board.

When she straightened, she shot Harry a triumphant grin. He wasn't smiling. He looked angry. Fine. His gaze lingered on her until part of her wanted to shout at him to stop it. At the same time, it had a hypnotic effect on her, and she couldn't seem to look away. She told herself it was nothing more than a contest of wills—to see who would blink first—and yet it didn't feel like that at all.

As the moment lengthened, Kate felt her cheeks redden and could have kicked herself. She hadn't blushed this hard in more than a decade.

Not since college, when she'd met Roddy. She'd been so lonely, so different than the other girls who seemed to know all the rules. And then Roddy had come along. He'd been a junior at the University of Virginia, and captain of the riding team. Without a doubt, he'd been the cutest boy Kate had ever laid eyes upon. From the moment he'd dared her to a cross-country race, she'd fallen for him.

Kate looked away from Harry, disgusted with herself. She tore another board loose. It felt wonderful to batter the old wood. Chips flew around her.

"Take it easy," Harry cautioned. "Short, targeted swings."

Her fingers tightened on the heavy metal tool. She wanted to take a short, targeted swing at his head. Another board tore loose, bringing with it part of the wooden framing beneath. *Now we're making progress,* Kate thought in satisfaction.

And then she felt the beam beneath her feet shift. At the same time, Harry leaped across the roof toward her shouting "Kate," and the board under her feet gave way completely.

She fell quickly and landed on her back in a pile of loose hay. For a moment she lay there, catching her breath and looking up at the sunlight pouring through the jagged hole. She shifted uncomfortably. Her legs felt pinned by a heavy tree. The tree, she realized, was Harry.

"Harry? You okay?"

He sat up and reached for his glasses which had fallen into the hay. "Yes, except that I fell on something hard, like a rock."

"That's my boot." Kate attempted to pull her foot loose from beneath his hip. "You're sitting on it."

As Harry shifted, Kate pulled her foot free.

"You okay, Kate?"

He had hay sticking out of his hair and enough straw coming out of his shirt to stuff a scarecrow.

"Yeah." She pulled a twig of straw from her mouth. "Why'd you jump across the roof? You knew the frame couldn't hold both of us."

Harry looked surprised. "I was trying to stop you from tearing out the framing." He shook his head. "You think I made us fall?"

Kate shrugged. "*Your* dive made the roof collapse."

"You were already falling. I tried to grab you."

Her chin went up a notch. "It felt like you pushed me, if you want the truth."

"Pushed you? I was trying to grab you despite the way you were swinging that crowbar."

She frowned at the lopsided grin on his face, and resisted the urge to straighten his glasses. "You have hay sticking out of your ear."

Harry removed a long strand of hay from behind her ear and offered it to her. "You think I have hay? You should see yourself."

What would she see if she did? Would the blush still be on her cheeks? Kate didn't want to answer the question. Didn't want to admit that after so many years, here she was again, sitting in hay with an attractive man and feeling herself tingle in a way that spelled nothing but disaster. *I can't go through this again, can't let him charm me and have him turn out to be as self-centered as his brother. It's not just me anymore—there's Jane to think about too.*

Almost as if he'd heard her, Harry released the strand of hay and it fluttered to the ground. "Come on," he said, rising. "Time to get back to work."

His fingers curled around her hand in a strong, steady grip as he pulled her to her feet. "I've got to go help get Jane get ready for school," she muttered, backing away.

She felt his gaze on her back as she nearly ran for the house. *Nothing's changed,* Kate told herself, taking his hand. *Nothing's changed between us,* she repeated. As she got to her feet, she sent a silent prayer skyward. *Please let the funny feeling in my stomach be nothing other than too many of my mother's blueberry pancakes.*

Chapter Six

Later that evening, Kate sank onto a bale of hay and listened to the sounds of the barn settling for the night. Normally the peaceful noises of horses munching hay or savaging their buckets for one last bit of grain filled her with contentment. Tonight, however, she fought a sense of panic. Time was running out. In less than a week, she would be in court and a judge would decide the future of her business. And if this wasn't enough, she couldn't even bear to think what would happen if Roddy sued her for joint custody of Jane.

"Want company?"

Kate looked up as Maureen walked down the aisle and, without waiting for an answer, plopped herself next to her. Maureen popped a can of soda and took a long swallow. "Your mother told me about what happened this morning," she said. "Listen, Kate, you and me are on the same page about Harry, but why don't you get his legal help, *and then* kill him off?"

Kate released her breath in a snort. "I'm not trying to kill anyone off. Besides, my mother already asked his legal opinion and it was a waste of time." She pulled a handful of hay from the bale and let it flutter to the floor. "My dad's strategy of boring everyone to death has more potential than anything Harry's come up with."

"Too bad. His brother may be a rat, but that's probably given Harry a lot of practice getting people out of trouble." She gave Kate a sideways look. "That and his looks. I'll bet any jury would give him anything he wanted."

"Right."

"I'm serious. He looks like Russell Crowe, only smarter."

"Oh for goodness sakes," Kate said. "Looks have nothing to do with the law."

"I don't know, Kate. Lawyers who wear custom-made shirts and Italian leather shoes don't lose many cases." She pointed her soda at Kate like a stylus. "He could be your secret weapon."

Kate frowned. "He's no legal weapon. More like a big, legal dud." She kicked the bail absently. "He's the most stubborn person I've ever met. Bossy too."

"He sounds an awful lot like you."

Kate crossed her arms around herself unhappily. "Just who does he think he is telling me I'm dangerous with tools?"

"He's right. You're the only person I know who can aim a can of oil at a door hinge and hit herself squarely in the eye."

"I'll never live that down." Kate dismissed Maureen's statement with a wave of her hand. "You're going to have to help me get rid of him."

"If you want him gone so badly, why don't you sign the divorce papers he brought?"

Frustration swelled in Kate. "I would, but they're not good anymore. Roddy never told him about Jane, and now he thinks I'm trying to deprive his brother of his parental rights."

A mouthful of soda sprayed from Maureen's lips. "That's the funniest thing I've ever heard in my life."

Kate nodded. "Funny or not, it's true. Now Harry won't leave until he's sure Roddy's rights are protected."

Maureen patted Kate's leg. "You aren't worried, are you? Roddy's not exactly the fatherly type."

"A little, mostly about what's going to happen to Jane. I don't trust Harry. What kind of person falls though a rotten roof *and* finishes the job?"

"I'm still here," Maureen pointed out. "You've done a lot worse to me over the years."

Kate laughed although it did little to loosen the band of worry around her heart. She knew Maureen was purposely trying to cheer her up. "You know what I mean."

Maureen spiked her short blond hair absently. "I don't know, Kate, but maybe he's legitimately interested in Jane. If so, it's possible he'll help you fight Simon now that it's a family thing. Besides, we could use the help more than you know."

Something about Maureen's expression made the back of Kate's neck prickle. "What do you mean, more than I know?"

"Oh nothing." Maureen studied her fingernail polish.

"Come on, Maureen. Spill it. Are you in trouble?"

"Not me, its Jimmy."

Ever since his divorce six months ago, Jimmy and Maureen had been dating. Jimmy ran a garage, and

Kate had assumed any day now Maureen would ride off happily into the sunset in Jimmy's tow truck.

"Jimmy's in trouble?"

"If I tell you, Kate, you have to promise to stay calm."

"Just tell me, and do it fast."

Across the aisle, a horse banged its feed bucket. Others munched the starchy hay. Kate braced herself against the back of the stall.

"When I learned about the problem with your divorce papers, I had Jimmy check his. It turns out the same judge—James T. Kirk—signed them as well." She paused. "In short, your uncle messed up Jimmy's divorce papers too."

Kate let the unwelcome news sink in slowly. She dragged her hands through her hair. "Uh oh."

Maureen shook her head. "Oh yes."

Kate squeezed Maureen's hand. "I never should have let Jimmy hire my uncle. Jeb's a great lawyer when it comes to mail-order estate planning, but it's been a while since he's handled anything else."

"It wasn't your fault. Jimmy needed a lawyer; your uncle needed a carburetor. Fate brought them together. The rest is history."

"History I'd give anything to change."

"What's past is past." Maureen's features hardened. "But we can change what's going to happen. Jimmy's wife doesn't want the divorce. It's going to be a battle all over again. If Jimmy and I are ever going to get together, we need a lawyer who is fearless. One who can fall through a roof in a single bound and—"

"That's leap buildings in a single bound. And Harry isn't Superman."

Maureen frowned. "He may not be Superman, but

he's better than your uncle. No offense, but sometimes I have to fight the urge to hold a mirror up to see if your uncle is still breathing."

"Jeb's a good lawyer," Kate defended her uncle automatically. "Still waters run deep, you know."

"Then Jeb's in over his head. Face it. We need help."

"We'll find a good lawyer."

"I think it could be Harry. We need to keep this in the family, otherwise your uncle could get into big trouble with the bar association."

"That's why we should keep Harry out of this. Besides, he's not family."

"He's Jane's uncle." Maureen narrowed her gaze at Kate. "That counts for something."

"With that family it counts for nothing." Kate heard her voice rising and found herself tearing up a blade of hay. "Have you forgotten everything that's happened?"

Maureen's eyes softened. "Of course not." She patted Kate's leg. "I just say it's time that family paid its dues." She smiled. "I say if he won't agree to help, we hold him hostage until he changes his mind." She winked so Kate would know she was trying to ease the tension between them. "My cuffs are in the car."

"Yeah," she agreed just to play along. "We'll dangle my mother's fudge brownies in front of him and offer him one for every page of brief he writes."

"Now you're talking."

Before Kate could reply, her mother came hurrying down the stable aisle toward them. "Have you seen Harry? He has a telephone call." She looked at Kate with anxious eyes. "It's the rat."

* * *

Harry looked up as Kate ran toward him. He wiped the sweat from his brow and leaned the sledgehammer against what was left of the lean-to. Frowning, he watched her come nearer, hair flying as she sped across the uneven ground and knee-high tawny grass.

Halfway across the pasture, she stopped and cupped her hands around her mouth. "Harry! You've got a phone call!" She motioned with her arm for him to come.

He headed toward her at a jog, all at once dreading the pending conversation with his brother. His words would change Roddy's life forever, not to mention the rest of the family's. One of the reasons he'd come in the first place had been to avoid a scandal. Now he had an even bigger bombshell to drop in their laps.

He followed Kate to Harlan's study and picked up the receiver. "Hello."

"You called?"

Harry twisted the receiver cord around his finger. *Congratulations Roddy,* he thought, *you're a father.*

"You there, Harry?"

Harry sank into Harlan's leather desk chair. "You sitting down?"

His brother laughed. "I take it Kate hasn't changed. She can still take a man's breath away. Be careful, bro, she doesn't give it back."

There wasn't any other way other than just to say it. "There's a child involved, Roddy. Kate says it's yours." He paused. "The girl looks an awful lot like you."

Harry closed his eyes and imagined his brother in Massachusetts absorbing the news. Although the line had gone dead quiet, he could hear the even pull of his brother's breath. "This changes everything," Harry spoke into the silence. "We'll add a custody arrangement to the divorce papers, of course."

"Hold it," Roddy said. "This is what I want you to do."

Ten minutes later, Harry hung up the telephone. For a moment, he simply sat staring at the instrument as if it was a valuable work of art he simply didn't understand. Even more baffling had been Roddy's reaction to his news. Over the years he'd represented a number of morally bankrupt clients, but none of them had inspired the sense of shame he felt now.

"Do you like barbeque ribs, Harry?" Prissy asked him as he walked out of Harlan's office. "It's an old Southern recipe. We slow-cook it—and, of course, baste it with the sauce every thirty minutes."

He nodded, barely registering the tantalizing smell of slow-cooked beef. Roddy's directives rang in his ears. He had an ethical obligation to carry them out and it conflicted with the moral obligation he felt as an uncle. He needed to think this through.

Following an impulse, he walked out of the house and followed the twisting path. The towering pines and slanting autumn light made it nearly impossible to see the ruts in the trail, but he didn't slow his pace.

He thought about his father, a lawyer who had started his own firm and built it into one of the most successful practices in Boston. His father had groomed him as his successor, both on a professional and personal level. Harry considered it his responsibility to look after his mother and brother, regardless of how he felt about their personal decisions.

This one stank, he thought, and walked further into the woods. What would his father have done? Carried out Roddy's wishes, or stood by his grandchild? Either way, a family member would be lost. It was an impossible choice.

He hiked up a hill and onto a long, flat rock that glittered the same silver color as a fish's scales, and where Kate knelt with her face lifted to the sky. Her eyes were closed and her lips moved in what had to be a silent prayer. For a moment, a thick beam of sunlight streamed over her, bathing her in a light that seemed almost spiritual.

Part of him wanted to turn away. He wasn't ready to face her, and had no desire to intrude on a private moment. Yet something in him would not let him leave, and compelled him to move even closer. His skin tingled with the impossible feeling that if he could turn his head quickly enough, he would see his father standing nearby. He could almost feel the warmth of his father's gaze in the autumn sun.

His father had liked Kate and hoped she'd be a steadying influence on Roddy. Unlike his mother, who'd wanted a bride with blueblood, not one who won blue ribbons at horse shows, and had looked down her nose at Kate, refusing to see the strength of character Harry's father insisted was there. Harry thought if his father could see Kate now, he would not be surprised to find her raising her daughter and running a riding academy.

A pebble crunched beneath his foot. Kate opened her eyes and saw him watching her. Turning to face him, she looked as hostile as any witness he'd ever cross-examined.

"I've spoken with my brother. He's instructed me on how to proceed." Harry hadn't known he would say this, and the words sounded stiff and formal to his own ears.

"Go ahead," Kate said. "What did the rat say?"

Harry wiped his glasses on his shirt. "It's like you said. He knew about Jane."

"And?"

"I'm authorized to offer you a settlement." Harry named a figure and watched the disappointment form in Kate's eyes. *So she wants more money,* he figured. *Good. This makes things easier.* "That number, of course, is contingent upon you and Jane staying out of Roddy's life. He doesn't want to hear from you ever again—and he doesn't want you contacting any other family members either."

Harry kept his features expressionless, although every part of his brother's instructions bothered him. "I'm having the papers drawn up. They'll be couriered here tomorrow for your signature."

Kate's hands went to her hips. "Don't bother. I'm not going to sign them."

Harry smiled without warmth. "If it's more money you want, I'm prepared to go higher." He named another sum.

Kate dropped her gaze and dug the toe of her boot against the rock. "It's not the money."

In Harry's experience, everything came down to dollars and cents. "Make a counter offer." He paused. "I probably shouldn't say this, but my brother is a wealthy man. We're talking Jane's future."

"Which is exactly why I'm turning down your proposition. I'm not signing any papers that make Jane seem like a dirty, little secret. She's a child, a wonderful, loving person."

Harry ignored the truth in Kate's words. His brother did consider Jane a dirty, little secret. He steeled himself to continue. "How will you pay for Jane's education? Where will you live if you lose the stable?"

Lifting her gaze, Kate met Harry's eyes. "I'm not accepting a penny from Roddy. The only thing he's capable of giving is heartache. I feel sorry for the woman he's going to marry."

Fascinated, Harry studied her closely. Was she serious, or merely holding out for more money? "If you feel that way, why not sign the settlement? That way you'd never have to deal with any of us, ever again."

Kate nodded. "If I never saw another Bond in my entire life, I'd be a happy woman. But that's not right for Jane."

"We're off the record here—but any court would award you child support no strings attached."

Kate put her hands on her hips. "How much do you want me to rub Jane's face in the fact that her father is a deadbeat dad?"

"You think she doesn't know that already?"

"I think she chooses to believe he's going to show up on our doorstep someday—just the way you did."

"And you're just as naive," Harry accused, "thinking that you don't need Roddy's money. My brother's settlement could help you make the repairs to the stable."

"For the last time, we won't be bought off." Kate set her jaw. "I'm not selling Jane's rights to know her entire family. Someday Jane is going to want to meet your side, especially now that she's met you. Jane has a right to be part of their lives—if and when she chooses."

Harry felt a bit like the devil trying to tempt her. "It's not blood money—its child support with a few stipulations."

"I won't take it," Kate stated flatly. She shook her head. "I want Jane to value things—like that Black-tailed Hawk circling over there, the smell of these pines, and the sound of my mom's Guinea hens. I want her to grow up counting her blessings—not her dollars. I want her to grow up surrounded by a family that values her and learning traits like compassion and kindness." She looked at him long and hard. "Why am I even explaining this to you? You couldn't possible understand." She turned then, and left him standing on the rock.

Harry watched her move through the trees until she disappeared from sight. Her words rang in his ears. He thought about his own life, and the things he valued most—his career, his condo, his investments. By anyone's measure, even his family's, he'd succeeded in life. Yet had any of these material things brought him lasting happiness?

He turned slowly and began to walk back toward the house. A rabbit zigzagged across the path in front of him. He noticed the way the tall strands of yellow grass bent and caught the light. The smell of rich earth filled his nostrils and felt cool and healing in his lungs.

As he neared the house, he saw the Guinea hens, funny looking birds with long, thin necks and twig-like legs. They squawked loudly when he approached, then scampered off in fear. Although he suspected they were quite stupid—he also wondered what lessons they had to teach. *Kate would know.*

Walking inside the house, he thought how different Kate was from any other woman he had ever met. She'd made him laugh with her ineptness with tools, baffled him with her lack of materiality, and touched him with her simple dignity. In the past twenty-four hours she'd shaken up his life more than anybody else had in thirty-four years. To his dismay, he realized, he liked it.

Chapter Seven

"Jane, hurry up!" Kate shouted the next morning. "You're going to be late for school." She filled a glass with orange juice and tried not to think about Harry, who continued to occupy her thoughts much more than she liked. Another sleepless night could easily be attributed to him.

"I'm here. I'm here." Jane said as she walked into the kitchen.

"Jane?" Kate's jaw dropped open.

Her daughter tugged the bottom of her T-shirt. "Morning, Mom."

Kate's eyes traveled down the bright pink T-shirt to the pair of cut-off denim shorts. Shorts in October? She frowned as her gaze traveled over her daughter's long, bare legs. Legs, she recalled, that had encircled a horse before she'd taken her first baby steps. She swallowed. When had her daughter started looking like a teenager?

"You're wearing shorts?" There had to be a terrible

mistake, and she intended to give Jane the benefit of the doubt. "It's freezing outside."

"No it isn't." Jane's chin lifted a fraction.

What in the world is going on? And is that her good luck necklace around her neck? The one Roddy had made her out of the nail of a horseshoe? All Kate had to do was look at that necklace and see herself, playing with fire, unprepared for the consequences.

It'd been a cold, October morning the day she met Roddy. They'd both been competing at a three-day event in northern Kentucky. Her horse had thrown a shoe during the warmup and she was desperate to find it, and a blacksmith. Instead, she found Roddy, who not only fixed both problems, but also, for luck, had shaped a horseshoe nail into a charm for her. He'd put it in the pocket of her riding coat. More than the blue ribbon she'd won that day, Kate remembered the heat of his fingers and the burning energy flowing from his gaze.

"Jane, is that my necklace?" Kate blinked back the memory as she reached for the metal charm. "You took it from my drawer?"

"You said I could borrow it." Jane's fingers gripped the twisted nail charm.

True enough, Kate had said that once, but years ago, when Jane had sat in her lap, back when Kate still believed Roddy would come for them.

"You can wear the necklace, but change your shorts. You need a sweater too."

"Mom, all my friends are wearing shorts today. We made a deal."

The challenge lay at Kate's feet. "If all your friends jumped off a cliff, would you?"

As soon as the words left her mouth, Kate winced.

She could have been her mother talking. Drawing her fingers through her hair, Kate wondered what other bits of her mother were imprinted in her brain.

"I'm not jumping off a cliff," Jane pointed out. "If I don't wear these shorts, none of my friends are going to talk to me."

"Then they aren't your real friends," Kate argued back, sounding exactly like her mother again.

"Mom, get real. What's the big deal?"

"It's October. Nobody wears shorts in New York in October."

"So?"

Kate's blood pressure shot even higher.

"It's completely inappropriate, not to mention they don't even fit you anymore."

"They fit great."

"Go change."

After shooting a dark stare at her, Jane turned and headed for the stairs. "You don't understand," she said in a dramatic tone of voice that suggested Kate had never been ten years old and couldn't possibly relate to any explanation she could utter.

Watching her go, Kate's heart ached for her daughter. Only too well she understood Jane's desire to be accepted by her friends. But shorts? It had to be some kind of ploy to gain attention. However, Kate feared the attention Jane would be getting would be from boys. First, she'd be content for them to look at her, next they'd be talking, and before she knew it, Jane would believe what they told her. That was the surest way to get hurt, Kate knew—trust someone who said he cared about you.

"Uncle Harry?"

Turning, Harry watched Jane charge toward him.

For a moment he thought something must be wrong for her to have left the house wearing shorts and a T-shirt.

Coming to stand before him, Jane grinned, broke a carrot and offered him half. "What are you doing?"

"Loading the wheelbarrow with lumber."

"Oh." Jane shivered in cool morning air.

"Cold?" Harry kept his voice neutral.

Jane shrugged. "All my friends are wearing shorts today." She imparted this piece of information with the air of untold importance.

"Nice." Harry's gaze returned to the remaining lumber. He hadn't slept well the night before, and hoped the physical labor would relax him.

"Aren't you curious why I'm wearing shorts?"

Harry had been a lawyer for too many years not to recognize a witness who wanted to talk. "You and your friends are up to something."

Jane's giggle told him he'd hit the nail on the head. Now he had to be careful not to seem too eager. If child-rearing was this easy, Harry wondered why everyone made such a big deal about it.

"I can't talk about it." Her eyes begged him to ask.

"Okay." Harry shrugged as if he could have cared less.

"It's a secret," Jane offered. When Harry didn't respond, she added, "Don't you want to know what the secret is?"

"I'm a lawyer." Harry hid a smile. "I hear lots of secrets."

"If I tell you, will you promise not to tell anyone?"

Rubbing his chin, Harry pretended to give the matter grave consideration. "Whatever a client tells me stays private. It's client-attorney privilege, sort of a nondisclosure agreement."

Jane's face brightened with understanding. "Oh. In that case, consider yourself hired."

Harry's head swung around in surprise. "Hired?"

"Yes," Jane assured him. "You're my lawyer now. I'm about to tell you a secret."

He nearly laughed aloud. Her logic was flawed, but impressive. Clients shared secrets with their lawyers. She told him a secret, therefore he was her lawyer. He reconsidered his earlier position on the ease of parenting.

In the distance, a small herd of horses grazed slowly, seemingly oblivious to the nip in the air that was quickly turning Harry's ears red.

Even Jane shivered. "The secret," she said, "is that the cool kids at school formed a new club. Me and my friends want to join. So we have to dress like this."

"It must be the pneumonia club to dress like this."

"Well, this is just the first stage," Jane defended quickly.

The girl shivered, and Harry fought the urge to drape his sweatshirt over her slight form. "Does your mother know about this club?"

"Of course not. It's part of the pact. I'm only telling you this because of the clothing part of being a lawyer."

The clothing part of being a lawyer. For the life of him, Harry couldn't fathom what she meant. "What are you talking about?"

"You know, the disclothing part. You can't tell anyone about what I'm wearing and why."

He laughed and would have continued laughing, if not for the slightly wounded look on Jane's face. He struggled to form an attentive look. "You mean the disclosure agreement?"

Jane nodded.

Thoroughly enjoying himself, Harry rested one foot against a pile of wooden planks. Jane was fresh and smart and pretty. He hated to think of her changing just to join a club. "Well, you know, you don't have to do everything this club tells you to."

Misunderstanding, Jane shook her head rapidly. "Of course I do. If I'm not part of the club, the cool kids will say mean things to me at recess."

The thought of girls ganging up on Jane had Harry frowning. He didn't like the idea of his niece being in this club, but he saw her point. To be singled out and picked on didn't sound like much fun either.

"What I'm saying, is that you can join the club without doing anything you don't want to do."

"Huh?" Jane looked at him with narrowed eyes.

"You have a lawyer now," Harry said. "We'll sue their ah, I mean, rear ends off if they don't let you in the club. It's called discrimination."

Jane appeared to give the matter a great deal of thought. "Thanks Uncle Harry, but I'd rather join the club just like everyone else."

"Okay. But remember, don't do anything you don't want to do."

"I won't. Wearing these clothes isn't so bad. Just wait until I tell you what you have to do next."

Warning bells went off in Harry's mind. He was beginning to grasp how little understanding of Jane's situation he had. "You better tell me about stage two."

Suddenly, Kate ran across the pasture toward them. "Jane," she said coming to a stop and slightly out of breath. "I've been looking for you. What are you doing still wearing those shorts?"

"I was teaching Harry how to feed the horses a carrot," Jane explained.

Kate's gaze swung to Harry, who shrugged.

In one hand, Kate held a backpack and matching lunchbox. With the other she pushed a yellow raincoat towards Jane. "It's going to rain any minute. Put this on."

"Talk to my attorney." Jane squeezed her arms tightly around herself.

Harry flinched as Kate shot him a look of disbelief. "You're her attorney?" She offered the coat to her daughter. "Take it or you're grounded."

Instead, Jane pointed to the entrance to the pasture. "Hey Mom, look at Houdini. He's trying to open the gate again."

Sure enough, over the top of Kate's head, Harry watched the pony bumping the gate. To his further disbelief, the pony seemed to be working the latch with its teeth.

"Houdini!" Kate screamed. She dropped the coat and charged across the pasture.

Through the trees at the end of the pasture, a flash of yellow appeared. Jane turned and ran for the bus stop. The raincoat lay in a heap at Harry's feet. With it, he noticed, was her lunchbox.

Picking up her lunch, Harry raced after Jane. For a ten-year-old, she ran fast. He could have called her back, but her headstart was a challenge he couldn't resist.

The air tasted cold and sweet, the way it had all those years ago on the mornings when he and Roddy had run from the summer cabin to the lake.

He hadn't thought about the icy plunge into Lake Tacoma for years, but the freshness of the morning and the pine needles under his feet brought everything back with a clarity that dissolved the years.

He remembered the thunk of his feet on the shaky wooden dock, and the triumphant cries as Roddy pushed off the edge, hung for a glorious instant in the air and then crashed beneath the surface of the water, only to rise sleek-headed and screaming.

He pushed the memory aside as he drew even with Jane. Ahead, the bus reached the stop and, with a blast of compressed air, flung open its door.

Harry pressed the lunchbox into her hands. The girl said, " 'Bye Uncle Harry," loudly enough to be heard by everyone inside the bus.

The driver grinned at him. "Nice stride, Uncle Harry," she said before the door whooshed closed.

The road curved and the bus disappeared from sight. He stood there for a moment, thinking about the pride he'd heard in Jane's voice when she'd called out to him. It touched something deep inside him that he hadn't known existed. It made him feel, well, important in a way that had nothing to do with how much money he made, or what famous people he could call clients.

He thought about how nimbly her mind worked, and the beauty of her smile. Kate's smile, he realized.

Turning, he headed toward Kate, who was hugging the Shetland pony as if it was a favorite child. She looked like a teenager in those slim-fitting jeans, and her hair blowing loosely around her shoulders. Watching her, he realized she loved that pony as much as if it was a champion thoroughbred. The pony stretched its neck over her shoulder and sniffed her pockets. To Harry, it looked like it was hugging her back.

He suddenly realized how much having Jane had changed Kate's life. She could have given up Jane for adoption and continued riding in competitions. If she had, her face, as well as his brother's, might now grace the same magazine covers. But she had walked away from it to come back here to an aging stable and aging parents and single parenthood.

His father had been right in the strength he'd seen all those years ago in her character.

Chapter Eight

Kate reached the shaggy, brown pony just before Houdini wriggled the latch open. Catching the worn leather halter, she pulled the pony's head away from the gate. "Houdini," she scolded gently. "I can't keep you cooped up in your stall all the time." She pointed to a pile of hay. "Why can't you eat hay like the other horses?"

Houdini simply returned her stare with one of amusement. The look told her he'd be working the gate latch again just as soon as her back was turned. She looked around for bailing twine to wrap around the gate and saw Harry racing after Jane with the coat and lunchbox in his hand.

She smiled at the sight, yet at the same time felt the familiar ache deep in her heart. She wished Jane had a father. Someone who made her feel important, and who loved her enough to run hellbent through an acre of rutted pasture just to make sure his daughter was neither cold nor hungry at school.

She watched them until they reached the school bus,

and Jane stepped on board. Even then, her gaze lingered as Harry waved until the bus disappeared around the turn. She did the exact thing each morning, and was oddly gratified for him to stand there in her absence.

Houdini nudged her, so she gave him the hug she'd wanted to give to Jane. He smelled like raw oats, fresh hay and sweet pony, and she loved it. The heaviness of his neck stretched over her shoulder in a pleasant weight. She instantly forgave him for being an equine escape artist.

As she tied the fence closed, it occurred to her that if Harry truly was interested in getting to know Jane, this could be good for them both. Other than her Grandpa and Jimmy, there were few men in Jane's life.

Still pondering what might be best for Jane, Kate headed for the lean-to. She wanted to check Harry's progress and see if there was enough wood to begin rebuilding the fence. When she reached the clearing, Kate saw the ribs of the shelter still standing and piles of lumber nearby. On closer inspection, she noticed Harry had sorted the wood by usability. He'd taken care to store the old nails in an old coffee container.

The way he'd systematically taken apart the old shelter told Kate that Harry valued organization, and careful attention to detail. He wasn't a bit like Roddy, who would have torn the structure down with gusto, leaving tools and materials scattered as if they were fallen soldiers on the battlefield.

Her gaze fell to the interior, now easily visible through the structure's skeleton. She remembered seeing Harry on the roof top, silhouetted by the trees and sky, and then how he had looked sprawled next to her in the hay. There had been a moment when Kate had looked at him and known they were both feeling the same tug of war between attraction and distrust.

Shaking her head at how narrowly she had avoided kissing Harry, Kate loaded a wheelbarrow with usable boards. A man like Harry probably had a multitude of girlfriends. Plus, if he was anything like his brother, he wasn't a stick-around type of guy.

She'd finished stacking the wheelbarrow when Harry came up behind her. "We made it," he said. "Lunchbox and raincoat."

He sounded so proud of himself she couldn't resist smiling. "Thank you for making sure Jane got safely on the bus."

He shrugged but didn't entirely eliminate the satisfied expression. "My pleasure."

She pushed the loaded wheelbarrow forward and Harry fell into step beside her.

"Jane's a great kid," he said. He gazed at the load of wood. "I'd offer to push that for you, but you'd probably run me over with it if I did."

She shot him a sideways glance, nearly topping the contents of the wheelbarrow in the process. "You're mighty chipper this morning. Do I dare ask why?"

"Your mother's blueberry pancakes," Harry replied. "I must have eaten ten of them."

"Only ten?" Kate teased.

"And bacon. I don't know how you stay so slim."

She felt his appreciative glance over her body and couldn't help the blush that burned her cheeks. What was it about him anyway? It wasn't like other men hadn't been interested in her before, hadn't complimented her looks or asked her on dates.

"You better keep your eyes on Houdini," she

warned. "He's following us. He likes buttons, remember?"

The pony wasn't that close, but her words had the desired effect. Harry stopped staring at her and glanced over his shoulder. "Walk faster, Kate," he urged. "That pony has his eye on me."

She giggled, sounding young and foolish, flirtatious even. The latter thought stopped her laughter short. The last thing she needed was for Harry to think she was coming on to him. However, when she glanced at him, he rolled his eyes in comic fear, and another series of giggles burst out of her. The wheelbarrow bounced over a rut in the path, nearly scattering the planks, as Harry urged her to move faster.

When they reached the gate, Kate set the wheelbarrow down and forced herself to stop watching Harry making faces at the pony and concentrate on opening the gate.

When finally the knots had been untied, Kate opened the entrance wide enough to allow Harry to push the load through, and then shut it as Houdini stretched his short neck hopefully over the top. She patted the pony's velvet-soft nose and planted a kiss between his wide-set eyes. "Be good," she urged him.

When she looked up, Harry met her gaze. Something like an ache went through her. "He's not a bad pony," she said, "sometimes he just wants attention."

Harry hefted the load of wood. "I know the feeling." He walked away, leaving her to study the way his back muscles flexed under the weight of the load, and the play of sunlight on his chestnut-colored hair.

"Wait a minute," she called and hurried after him. "You don't have to help fix the fence, you know." She reached his side. "I'm not about to change my mind about what I said yesterday." He didn't slow his pace or look at her. "I don't want anything to do with Roddy's settlement or his stipulations either."

Harry kept walking. "I didn't expect you to change your mind. Although I don't agree with you, I'm not about to force you to take Roddy's money."

Frowning, Kate shot a sideways look at him to make sure he wasn't up to something. "You won't?"

Harry shook his head. "Last night, I thought a lot about what you said, and I am not going to fight you on this. We're going to do it your way—a straight custody arrangement. The courier should be here by ten tomorrow morning."

"Good. Very good." Kate hesitated, debating mentally before speaking. "If you want to stay in contact, with Jane I mean, after you leave, that'd probably be okay."

They reached the gravel parking area. Harry set the wheelbarrow handles down and wiped his glasses on his shirt. He met Kate's gaze. "I'd like that," he said.

She swallowed. A warm breeze lifted the strands of her hair off her shoulders. She could almost feel Harry's gaze doing the same thing to something deep inside her. As the moment lengthened, she could almost feel the years slipping backward and a weight disappearing from her shoulders. It was almost as if she was eighteen again, meeting a man's gaze for the first time, and feeling as if the moon and the stars were within her reach.

She didn't look away, not even when she felt his shadow fall over her. She smelled the faint odor of freshly washed cotton mixed with a heavier, definitely male smell. It made her think of clean sheets air-drying in the sun, and herself, as a child, pulling the smooth fabric tightly around her, filling herself with the heavenly smell.

Somewhere in the barn a horse whinnied and Kate stepped backward, putting more distance between them. Harry quickly turned back to the wheelbarrow, and then made a great show of readjusting the planks in it.

What had almost happened between them? Kate didn't know whether to be horrified or disappointed that they'd nearly kissed. She pushed her hair back. *What is the matter with me? Don't I have enough complications in my life right now without adding a man to them?*

Neither spoke until they reached the fence. Harry set the load down and looked past her to the fence. "This isn't going to look so pretty." He rolled his sleeves. "The wood isn't going to match and it'll be pretty uneven."

"I don't care how ugly it is," Kate declared, not quite looking at him either. What she felt for Harry was purely physical, nothing more. Attractions were like ghosts. All a person had to do was tell herself they didn't exist and eventually they would go away. "As long as it's forty-eight inches high, I'll be happy."

Still addressing the fence, Harry rested his hands on his hips. "We'll need a post digger, of course."

Kate studied the fence post. The only danger in an attraction was mistaking it for something it wasn't. "Can't we just add to its height?"

"We could," Harry agreed, "but it'll fall over if we do. We're adding to the weight the fence has to hold, remember?"

Kate set the post into the ground and kicked dirt into the hole. "Can't we just brace the post with some rocks?"

Without replying, Harry pushed the post with his index finger. It immediately leaned at an alarming angle. "The post wasn't set deeply enough to begin with."

Kate sighed, unhappy the repair work would be more complicated than she'd planned, but relieved to get away from him. "Okay. There's a post digger in the tool shed. I'll go get it."

When she returned a few minutes later, Harry and the big black dog were playing catch. Engrossed in their game, neither saw her. Harry pitched the ball, and Georgie's long legs scrambled comically to retrieve it. She could swear he and Georgie wore identical expressions of pleasure. *Oh Lord, did he have to like dogs too?*

Later that night, Kate lay in bed. Although her muscles ached pleasantly from working on the fence, and the room was dark and peaceful, she couldn't sleep. Moonlight filtered through the curtains and outlined the shape of the dog, Georgie, who sprawled across the foot of Kate's bed.

She hadn't spoken a word in hours, but both of them knew the other was awake. Kate felt the dog watching her with an intentness that seemed almost telepathic. She gazed up at the ceiling, where Harry slept in the room above her.

She couldn't help but think about the odd symmetry that had developed between them as they repaired the fence. It had felt like a friendship—he certainly hadn't held back teasing her about her ineptitude with tools—and yet there had been those moments when their hands had touched and her entire body tingled. Once he'd stood behind her, encircling both her and the fence post with his arms, and only a hair's-breadth of distance separated them. It had taken everything in her not to close that distance. Only the knowledge that Harry was Roddy's brother had enabled her to pretend his proximity had no effect on her.

Flipping onto her side, Kate looked out the window. She thought about Jane's inappropriate clothing. Her daughter probably had worn the outfit to get attention—Harry's attention. She knew the desire for a father's approval burned deep and fierce within her daughter. Somehow she'd have to make Jane understand that she couldn't count on Harry to fill that need, and that this was no fault of Jane's.

She worried about her uncle as well. He'd finally returned her phone calls, but had been as baffled as she about the divorce papers. He'd spoken directly to the judge, he'd explained, who had explained how to handle everything through the mail. He hadn't forged anything. Pulling out the old file, Uncle Jeb had even given her a telephone number of Judge James T. Kirk. Kate intended to call that number first thing in the morning. No wonder she couldn't sleep, Kate decided, with all there was to think about.

She shifted again, pulling herself into a sitting position. In the dark room, the dog's eyes gleamed like moonlight on water. She had the odd feeling Georgie knew exactly what she had been thinking. The dog also sat up and grinned at her, further giving the impression of unspoken understanding.

I know why you can't sleep, the dog seemed to say to her. *And that reason is sleeping in the room right above your head. The question is: What are you going to do about it?*

After a long moment, Georgie jumped off the bed

and padded softly out of the room. Kate listened to the creak of the stairs as the dog headed for the same place she'd been going for the past several nights.

She heard the distant squeak of hinges as the big dog pushed open the door. *Traitor,* Kate thought, *she's probably snuggling next to Harry at this very minute.* Pulling the covers more tightly around herself, Kate resigned herself to another sleepless night.

Chapter Nine

The courier arrived just before 10 o'clock the next morning. Harry gave the post a final blow with the sledgehammer and wiped his hands on his sweatpants. Harlan's sweatpants actually. Prissy had lended him the clothing while she washed his.

A few feet away, Kate nailed an extension to a fence post. With her lower lip caught between her teeth, and a cap turned around backwards on her head, she looked more like a teenager than the mother of a ten-year-old. He didn't have the heart to tell her she'd attached the board to the wrong side of the post.

Barking mightily, as if they were under attack, Georgie ran flat out to the parking area as a white van pulled into the lot. Only her wagging tail gave away her intention of greeting, not biting the driver.

From the side of the parking lot, a group of Guinea hens began screeching their disapproval in a series of earsplitting shrieks that rose in long, discordant bursts against the incessant barking of the dog.

Leaning his tool against the repaired structure,

Harry shot Kate a sideways glance. "Looks like my courier is here. We better rescue him before your animals scare him off."

"Yeah," she said, but made no move toward the parking lot.

His feet didn't want to move either. Instead he looked at Kate, trying to read her mood. Was she reluctant to see him go? He wanted to ask, but feared she'd treat the question like a joke. Certainly, he would if the situation was reversed. Silence was better than the flippant response he imagined.

He studied her face. The dark circles under her eyes told him that she hadn't slept any better than he had. Although he liked to tell himself that Georgie snored, deep inside he knew his inability to sleep had nothing to do with the Newfoundland. It had everything to do with the woman in front of him. That she might feel the same poked at him, destroying the sense of closure the arrival of the courier represented.

"We'd better go," Harry said, because he wouldn't let himself ask the question that nagged at him.

"Before the courier leaves," Kate finished for him.

He watched her stride briskly away, and admired the curve of her pockets across the back of her tight denim jeans. When had he last spent time with a woman who wore anything but dryclean only? But it was more than the swing of her hips that drew him to her. There was something elementally good within her. He'd seen it when she hugged her daughter; when she lifted her face in prayer; even when she kissed that stupid, button-eating pony. Heck, he wished she'd look at him as if she saw something wonderful inside him.

The courier remained inside the white van until

Kate hauled Georgie away from the door. Stepping outside, the man glanced fearfully at the Guinea hens, who continued to squawk from a safe distance. "Mr. Bond?"

"That's me."

"Here's your package."

Harry took a fat, sealed envelope from the man's hands. "Thank you."

"You want me to wait?" The driver gave the Georgie an anxious glance.

Shaking his head, Harry motioned the man away with a wave of his hands "No thanks. I'll be bringing this back myself."

"Okay then," the driver said. In two steps he was back inside the van, and seconds later it roared out of the parking lot.

Harry turned to Kate. "The new papers are here. Shall we go inside and take a look at these?"

Releasing the dog, who immediately jumped up to sniff the envelope, Kate straightened. "Might as well."

He looked at the envelope in his hand. A small streak of dog goop darkened the corner where Georgie had sniffed it. These documents were the reason why he had come in the first place, yet suddenly they were an unwelcome weight in his hand. Harry tightened his grip. After Kate signed these, he could be on his way back to Boston.

As they walked inside the stable office, he reminded himself that his law firm was where he belonged. Soon he'd be docking his laptop into its station and disappearing into an ordered world, where work dominated his waking hours, and no big dogs snuck into bed with him.

Harlan glanced up from the battered, metal desk.

The smile of welcome faded at the sight of the official-looking envelope in Harry's hand. His gaze traveled to his daughter, and then back to Harry, who felt like the villain in an old movie despite the fact that he'd done nothing wrong.

"Guess I'll be checking on the horses," Harlan said and left.

Alone with Kate, Harry skimmed the documentation. Satisfied the contents contained all the information he'd dictated, he passed the papers to Kate. "It's all here, exactly as you wanted it."

She read through the papers, nodding thoughtfully. When she reached the part where her signature was required, she glanced up, her expression unreadable. "This looks good." With a flourish, she signed her name at the places indicated and handed him back the papers.

Harry found himself oddly reluctant to take the documents, and even less anxious to admit to himself his business with Kate was finished. He shifted his weight and let his gaze travel across the papers on the desk. Reading upside down, he saw Judge Kirk's name and phone number. It reminded him that he still had one piece of unfinished business. "Did you ever ask your uncle why he forged the initial divorce in the first place?"

Kate toyed with the scrap of paper. "Yeah. It was all an innocent mistake, just like I thought."

"Just when is forgery an innocent mistake?" He held his hand up at Kate's protest. "You can relax, I'm not filing charges against him."

Kate sighed. "Well, he thought he was following the judge's instructions, but his hearing isn't that good." She glanced at the paper. "Apparently, he wrote down the wrong phone number, so we didn't actually speak to a real judge."

"Whom did he speak to?"

"Let's just say someone in the janitorial department of the New York Supreme Court has a very warped sense of humor."

He saw the strain in her smile, and wanted to put his hand on her shoulder. "Well it's all straightened out now."

Before Kate could answer, the door to the office banged opened and Maureen Reilly and a short man with linebacker shoulders stepped inside.

"Kate!" The tall blond wore her police blues and an expression of extreme agitation. Her companion planted himself next to her, spreading short but muscular legs, and shooting Harry a look that in one glance established him as both boyfriend and bodyguard.

Harry met his glance without blinking. He had no argument with this muscle-bound friend of Maureen's. His only concern was for Kate, who obviously was about to be on the receiving end of what appeared to be a major crisis.

"Kate, thank goodness you're here," Maureen said. "We need to talk."

"What's the matter?" Kate glanced at Harry, who purposely stepped closer to her, and drew himself a little straighter. He might not have the body of a football player, but if it came down to it, he had a damn good right hook.

"Bonnie is in danger," Maureen announced.

"Bonnie is in danger," Kate repeated slowly. "Maureen, what are you talking about?"

Who is Bonnie? Harry had the feeling that he'd better leave before he found out. Yet he couldn't seem to move. It was like driving past an accident and not being able to look away.

"Jimmy's cousin just called. Carla came to his garage and had him put a trailer hitch on the back of her Suburban. She told him she was about to take a trip."

"Carla is Jimmy's ex-wife," Kate explained.

Okay. Carla is Jimmy's ex-wife, so Bonnie must be their daughter. But why was it such a big deal for her to put a trailer hitch on her car? Harry stopped himself. He'd finished his job here.

"So maybe she's going camping," Kate suggested. "That doesn't sound like something to get upset about."

"She doesn't own a camper," Maureen said loudly. "Can't you see what she's planning? She's going to stick Bonnie in a trailer and kidnap her."

"She's never gotten over losing her in our divorce," Jimmy pointed out. "Maureen and I drove past her house and saw a brand new trailer in her driveway. My cousin thinks she might be leaving tonight."

Maureen patted the pistol in her holster. "Well, she isn't going anywhere. We're spending the night guarding Bonnie."

"Don't even think of doing that." Kate's gaze swung from Maureen to Jimmy. "Somebody will get hurt."

Maureen's chin lifted. "I can handle this."

"You're too personally involved," Kate pointed out. "If Carla does come, seeing her ex-husband with you is only going to make things worse."

"We aren't planning on shooting anyone." Jimmy glanced at Maureen. "Are we?"

"Of course not." Maureen's lips formed a wry smile. "Well, not on purpose anyway."

"Great." Kate groaned. "It's not enough that my daughter has gone to school wearing shorts in October, an injunction has been filed against my business, but now my best friend wants to play gunfight at the OK Corral in my barn." She put her head in her hands.

"Kate, are you okay?" Harry tried to read the set of her shoulders.

"The thing is," Jimmy insisted, "if we don't do something, Carla is going to kidnap Bonnie tonight."

"You don't know that," Kate said from behind her hands.

"I lived with this woman for ten years," Jimmy said. "She microwaved the goldfish just because I liked it."

"Don't worry." Maureen patted her gun again. "Nothing's going to happen to Bonnie."

"Put that away." Kate rubbed the skin on her face. "You know how I feel about guns." She sighed. "Bonnie will be safe in the barn, but if you'd feel better, I'll stay with her tonight."

Harry frowned. *What is it about the woman that she has to look after everyone? Who looked after her?*

It wasn't any of his business what Kate did, Harry told himself. He'd made a career out of not caring, not getting personally involved. He'd veered from that strategy once, and looked what had happened. In less than forty-eight hours he'd fallen through a roof and ended up rebuilding a fence.

"You have Jane," Maureen pointed out. "I'm the professional here. The minute I point my gun at Carla, she'll drop like a fly."

"I wouldn't bet on that." Jimmy shrugged apologetically. "She's stronger than she looks."

Harry surprised himself by blurting out, "Oh, for goodness sakes, get a restraining order."

Maureen reacted first. A smile stretched across her narrow face, softening the harsh planes of her cheek-bones and revealing the softness of her nature Harry had not seen before.

"Brilliant. Why didn't I think of that?" She looked at Harry. "Now all we need is a lawyer who can fill out the paperwork." She looked straight at Harry.

I'm not getting involved with this, Harry decided. *It probably was a child custody issue, although how it involved Kate's stable I'm not sure.*

"This is absurd," Kate stated. "We don't need a re-straining order."

"She's not a nice woman, Kate." Maureen patted her holster. "If you try to stop her, she might try and hurt you."

"What about you?" Kate said. "You're a meter maid. Not Dirty Harry."

"You think being a meter maid is easy?"

"Wait a minute," Harry said. "Fighting with each other isn't going to solve anything." He looked at Kate's blotchy face and exhausted eyes and heard himself say, "Look, I'll write up a motion for a restraining order. If she shows up, wave it at her, and call the police."

"I'm the police," Maureen reminded him with tri-umph in her voice.

"And the last person who should get involved with this," Kate said, "especially when Jimmy is going to have to refile for divorce."

He definitely didn't want to get involved with an-other faulty divorce. Some other lawyer could fill out the restraining order against Jimmy's ex-wife. They didn't need him. Harry glanced down at Kate's tightly clasped fingers. Bare of rings, slender and white, they seemed vulnerable and fragile, like Kate herself, which no one seemed to see except himself. Before he could stop himself, he reached for the pad of paper.

"Okay, I'll do it. Just give me Bonnie's full name and address."

Maureen pushed a blank pad into Harry's grasp. "Bonnie B. Good."

Pen in hand, Harry paused. It was all so obvious now. If he hadn't been so busy worrying about Kate he would have seen it sooner. "We're protecting a *horse*?"

"A ten-year-old sorrel beauty." Jimmy's voice rang with pride.

"We're writing a restraining order on behalf of a horse." Harry looked at the paper in disgust.

Jimmy shot Kate an impressed look. "He's fast. Catches on much quicker than Jeb."

"I like you, Harry," Maureen announced. "You're not like your turd of a brother." A thought seemed to occur to her, and for a moment she looked at Harry more closely. "You are a real lawyer, aren't you?" Before Harry could answer, she waved her hand. "Actually, don't tell me. I don't care."

Pulling Jimmy by the elbow, Maureen led him out of the office. "Come on Jimmy. We've got to let Harry get to work." She grinned at Kate. "And we didn't even have to tie him down."

After they'd gone, Harry turned to Kate. "You don't need a lawyer; you need an entire legal department."

Kate crossed her arms on her chest. "It isn't always like this."

Harry's dark eyebrows rose. "Your pony trespasses, your dog steals golf balls, and now you've got a SWAT team strategizing in your barn."

Kate bristled. "I guess you think this is hilarious."

He gave her a sharp look. "Not as much as any judge would think if I presented a restraining order on behalf of a horse." He crumbled the paper. "I'm not sleeping in a barn to stop a horse-napping, either."

"I wouldn't dream of asking."

"Good." Harry pushed his glasses higher on his nose. "Because I'm going back to Boston *today*."

"I can see that you certainly can't stay."

"A man would have to be absolutely crazy to hang out in a barn with a group of people with more firing power than Rambo."

"You're absolutely right. I'm completely capable of taking care of everything myself."

"Oh, heck. Who are you fooling? Somebody has to save you from yourself." He let his breath out slowly. "I'm staying."

Chapter Ten

"Kate?" Harry nudged her leg with his foot.

"What?" She jerked on the plaid woolen horse blanket that covered the stall floor. Moonlight spilled through a small window at the back of the stall, illuminating the rough contours of Harry's face.

"How many divorces do you think your uncle handled?"

She sighed. "Just two—mine and Jimmy's. Mostly, he helps people write their wills and provides estate counseling over the internet."

"That's a relief. I was wondering who else was going to pop up and need your help." He paused. "By the way, what did Maureen mean when she said something about tying me up?"

Playing bodyguard to Jimmy's mare with Harry wasn't turning out to be a very good idea, Kate decided. She pulled her knees more tightly to her chest, trying to keep more distance between them. Did the night have to be so clear? The barn so cozy? Even hay reeked of sun and shadow, earth and sky.

"She didn't mean anything," Kate replied at last.

"She meant something."

With Maureen, the idea had seemed humorous. Here in the barn with no one but horses for a chaperone, it didn't seem so funny anymore.

"We were joking around." Kate hoped the darkness hid the color in her cheeks. "We figured if we tied you down and bribed you with my mother's fudge brownies, we could get you to help with Jimmy's divorce."

His chuckle was a deep, rich noise that seemed to vibrate inside her chest. Kate closed her eyes. *I'm not seventeen anymore. I'm older, wiser, and heaven help me, incredibly attracted to this guy.*

The blanket shifted as Harry moved closer to her until he sat right next to her. Kate could not bring herself to open her eyes. She tried remembering the promises Roddy had made in the dark, promises she had been only too willing to believe. As a young woman, she'd been star-struck in love, blindly giving pieces of herself. All she'd wanted was for Roddy to love her. She'd believed with all her heart that if she made him happy enough, he would.

"Do you always do this?" Harry seemed even nearer. His voice was close enough to tickle her ear.

"Do what?"

"Rescue everyone. Since I met you, you've been like a one-woman disaster recovery team."

"Of course not." Kate tried to keep her voice steady and ignore the hum of blood in her veins. She stared straight ahead and forced herself to keep the conversation light. "We all try and look after each other, which is probably what causes the problems in the first place."

They sat in silence for a moment listening to the

sounds of horses settling down for the night. There was a rustle of hay, a splash of water, a dull thud of a horse lying down. Kate's heart beat faster.

"Why did you stay tonight, Harry?"

"I'm trying to help you, although it seems like a hopeless task."

I am hopeless, Kate thought. *Here I am, up to my neck in problems and all I think about is kissing Harry.*

"Harry?"

"Yeah?"

She swallowed. "Nothing."

Harry's fingers lifted and lightly tucked a strand of hair behind her ear. It wasn't like the touch of the breeze Kate had once imagined his touch would feel like. His fingers moved across her cheek lightly, but his fingertips were wonderfully rough. *This was the catch*, Kate realized, *to feel this way*. All the walls she had so carefully constructed around herself suddenly seemed flimsy, rendered unstable by one soft caress. "Where did you get this tiny white scar?"

She closed her eyes as his fingers traced the small white mark at her hairline. "Sawing a branch."

Harry gave a low, deep chuckle and continued to touch her face. "You and tools," he said.

Just once, she promised herself, she'd let her guard down. She'd let herself forget he was Roddy's brother. Slowly she lifted her hand. With trembling fingers she traced the swirl of hair behind his ear, the edge of his jaw bone. Her eyes remained shut and her lips parted softly.

She hadn't learned anything at all. Here she was ten years later, hellbent on repeating her mistakes as surely as if she had been given a script. Yet she didn't have the strength to draw away. She didn't want to try.

He closed the distance between them. His mouth covered her lips and his breath felt warm and moist on her cheek. His arms branded around her, pulling her against him and holding her in a grip that should have been painfully tight, but instead seemed to be the only thing holding her together.

His lips explored the shape and taste of her mouth, and something in Kate gave up the last threads of hope that she could simply stand up and walk away from the kiss anytime she chose.

Her longing unfolded within her like the petals of a flower opening to the sun, revealing at last that Roddy had broken nothing inside her. Her heart beat strong and true, and every pull of breath confirmed the rebirth of emotions she'd long considered dead. With a sense of wonder, she felt the unfamiliar contours of Harry's body finding a fit against her own, reshaping them both into one incredible being.

Never, she realized distantly, had she experienced anything like this, and she doubted she ever would again. The closeness to Harry had to be God-given. It was like the seams of their souls had ripped open to fit against each other. Even in her wildest dreams she'd never imagined she could feel like this.

Any minute now, Harry would want to close the last of the spaces between them. When that happened, she wondered if she would have the strength to pull away.

Somewhere in the distance, a horse scraped the ground as it swung itself to its feet. The noise repeated itself through the barn until Kate couldn't ignore it anymore. And then she heard footsteps.

"Do you hear that?" Kate whispered.

Harry kissed her neck. "Hear what?"

"Something," Kate whispered. "Listen."

"It's my heart," Harry replied softly. "You hear what you're doing to me."

The sound of footsteps grew louder. "It's not your heart. It's footsteps. Carla's coming."

Harry pulled back as the unmistakable tap of shoes on the concrete aisle grew louder. "Someone's coming."

Kate covered her mouth. "Oh no, I feel like laughing."

"Pull yourself together."

The footsteps clicked closer. Harry's hand reached to the bale of hay where Maureen had laid out the weaponry. His hand closed around the baseball bat. Kate grabbed a flashlight and a curled rope.

The footsteps stopped outside Bonnie's stall, and a beam of light pierced the darkness. Harry reached for Kate's free hand. They quietly opened their stall door.

The bolt slid back on Bonnie's stall.

"Stop!" Harry raised the bat as the beam from Kate's flashlight illuminated the intruder.

A tall woman in a tan trench coat gasped in shock. She lifted her arm as if she intended to throw something at them. Kate glimpsed a red apple in her hand.

Harry stepped forward. "Just hand me the apple, nice and easy, and nobody gets hurt."

Kate smothered another giggle. He sounded absurd, like someone on a bad police show.

Carla angled nervously away from Harry until her back pressed against the side of the stall next to Bonnie's. "This isn't what you think," she said.

An old mare, Nanna, lifted her head from the hay

and stared with interest at the sound of Carla's voice. Her nose twitched at the scent of apple.

Kate stepped forward. "We know you're here to steal Bonnie. Now hand over that apple."

"Are you crazy?" Carla laughed nervously. "I'm not here to steal Bonnie, just to feed her an apple." She opened her fingers to reveal the fruit. "I wanted to be sure Jimmy wouldn't be around when I came. That's why I'm here so late."

"Sure Carla, that's why you got a new trailer hitch on your Suburban." Kate extended her hand. "You're trespassing and I'm calling the police."

"You don't understand," Carla said. "I'm not here to hurt Bonnie. I'm trying to say good-bye." She took a couple of steps back, and clutched the apple to her chest. "I'm moving to Syracuse. I bought the trailer to move some furniture."

A dark shape loomed behind Carla, but before Kate could shout a warning, the old mare lunged for the apple.

Nanna's long neck cleared the side of the stall, but the combination of near blindness in one eye and Carla's movements made the horse misjudge her swing. There was a loud cracking sound, like two stones banging together, and then, soundlessly, Carla fell to the ground.

Harry stepped forward and peered at the woman on the ground. "My God. I think she's dead."

Kate, already kneeling by Carla, found a pulse in her throat. "She isn't dead, just knocked out. Call nine-one-one."

Later, after the ambulance had taken Carla away, Harry and Kate walked back to the house.

"Go ahead and say it," Kate said. She looked down at the path and sidestepped a large rock.

"Say what?"

"That our stable needs an entire legal department to support us."

Harry paused. He looked up at the stars and moon half-hidden behind the clouds. "I wasn't even thinking that," he said. "Although, you have a point there."

In the distance, Kate heard an owl hoot and shivered. It didn't seem like a good omen. "She hardly lost consciousness," she said. "Couldn't have been more than ten minutes before she woke up, and she seemed perfectly coherent."

"She was coherent," Harry agreed. "For a woman who had just been bludgeoned in the head by a horse."

"I'm sure she'll feel better in the morning." Kate tried not to think about the look of outrage in Carla's eyes as the ambulance attendants wheeled her away. "Maybe she'll forget the whole thing."

"A woman who was asking for her lawyer as she was carried out on a stretcher isn't likely to forget," Harry pointed out. "She's going to sue you."

"Even though she was the one trespassing?"

"She was injured on your property by your horse. Legally, she's entitled to fill out a personal liability claim," Harry replied. "It doesn't mean she'll win."

A cloud passed over the moon, eclipsing the small circle of light. Kate shivered again. She crossed her arms on her chest, hugging herself hard, trying to hide the way her hands trembled.

Seeming to sense her distress, Harry dropped his arm around her shoulders. "At least you didn't kill her."

She heard the smile before she saw it. The heat of his arm warmed her, almost immediately taking away the chill of the night air. His arm felt so strong, capable, and dependable. For a moment she let herself lean into him, imagining what it would be like to let herself depend on him. Pure heaven. But what if the going got tough? Would he stick it out?

The thought sobered her up. She ought to shrug off his arm around her, throw her shoulders back and concentrate on being strong and independent. Kissing Harry had been a moment of weakness, but standing here under the stars with him, wanting to kiss him again, was nothing short of insanity.

The silence stretched between them. She couldn't even remember what he had just said. Above, stars glittered in a black velvet sky, seeming to promise treasures for those brave enough to try and grab them. Kate didn't feel very brave, or even daring enough to lift an arm.

"What am I going to do now?" Her voice was barely louder than a whisper.

When Harry didn't reply, she wondered if he had even heard her.

"We're going to court," Harry stated. "I'll help you."

Chapter Eleven

S*ome legal dream team*, Harry thought, looking around at the group assembled in Kate's kitchen. It was Friday evening. He had only two days to prepare for the trial. *It's sort of like Don Quixote and family versus Saddam Hussein. How can we possibly win this case?*

Still, they were all he had and there wasn't much time. He cleared his throat to get their attention.

"Let's get started." He looked around the table at the hopeful faces. *Just business as usual*, he told himself, only it wasn't. He'd never defended a client he'd kissed. He couldn't even look at Kate without wanting to kiss her again.

He cleared his throat more for his benefit than anyone else's. "We're here to prepare the Withers' defense for the final hearing to determine if the injunction against their business will become permanent."

"We should be preparing an ironclad trust fund for Jane," said Jeb Withers, who added another spoonful of sugar to his coffee and stirred vigorously. "I've been working this case since the beginning. We've got to tie everything up so Simon can't get it."

"Mr. Withers," Harry began, "you can't fight these people with nothing more than an updated will."

Jeb blinked furiously. "I'm talking more than a will. We'll bury assets all the way to China if we have to. I'm talking setting up an ironclad trust fund."

He said the last words almost reverently. Harry drew his hands through his hair. "I think we can do more than that." The conviction in his voice surprised him.

Jeb pulled at his thick white mustache. "They have resources that we can't begin to compete against. Half the judges in the county belong to Simon's golf club, and the other half wish they belonged."

Meeting the older man's gaze, Harlan said, "Don't worry, Harry is an expert in matters like these."

Harry tried not to smile. His firm specialized in enterprise alliances, not small businesses, and particularly not those where animals had been named in the grievance.

"Consider me nothing more than a resource." Harry smiled into the older men's eyes. "Since I'm not licensed in New York, you'll need to plead the case."

Jeb raised one eyebrow in suspicion, reminding Harry strongly of a look Kate gave him all too often. However, Jeb seemed pleased to hear that he still was needed. "Let's hear your plan."

Night had fallen so completely that it was as if someone had taped black paper over the windows. Yet the kitchen blazed with light, and a fire crackled in a friendly sort of way from the family room fireplace.

"I have assignments for everyone." Harry flipped

through a thick pad of notes. "We've got a lot of ground to cover and not a lot of time." He tapped his pen thoughtfully against the pad. "Harlan, you've already done research on the riding academy's history. Now I'd like you to put some numbers together on your safety record."

"No problem." Harlan's eyes lit up at the prospect of plowing through the record books. "I've kept a very thorough diary of events."

Next, Harry turned to Prissy. "I want you to check with the historical society and look into the possibility of registering the farm as a historical landmark."

"Got it." Prissy picked up a plate. "More fudge brownies, Harry?"

Harry couldn't resist choosing the largest one.

"This is a waste of time." Jeb tapped his hearing aid.

"If the farm is classified as a historical landmark," Harry explained, "it might not be subject to the same laws and restrictions as if it's classified as a working farm."

"The grandfather clause won't hold when there are charges of endangerment," Jeb argued. "If its animals endanger people, it's a hazard to the general public and subject to the same rules and regulations."

Harry waved his hand. "We can throw case after case study where entertainment businesses have had accidents. It's what insurance is for. We'll also counterattack," he continued, "that's where you, Jimmy, come in."

"Me?"

"Your towing business gives you industry contacts. Find out how many windshields have been smashed by golf balls in the past year."

"No problem." Jimmy cracked his knuckles as if he relished the prospect of extracting this information by violence if necessary.

"How about me?" Maureen practically vibrated in her seat with excitement. "What do you want me to do?"

With her police contacts, Harry had figured she would be an invaluable resource. Now, however, looking at the gleam in her eye, he wondered if she wasn't a little too excitable. "We're putting you on Simon. Run him through the police computer, and find out everything you can. He'll have a weak area. It's just a matter of finding it."

He watched Maureen fix a triumphant glance at Kate. "I told you that scumbag Simon is hiding something. Starting tonight, I'm putting him under twenty-four-hour surveillance."

All too easily Harry imagined Maureen getting arrested for stalking Simon. "Be careful," he warned. "Whatever you do, don't let him know you're investigating him."

Jane spoke for the first time. "What about me? What's my job?"

Harry nearly smiled at the fierce determination in her eyes. She was a fighter, like her Mom. What task could he give her to make her feel useful? Stroking his chin thoughtfully, he considered the girl's strengths. "You'll get character witnesses for the animals named in the injunction."

Jane's dark eyebrows drew together thoughtfully. "What do you mean?"

"Houdini, Georgie, and the Guinea hens have been declared a public nuisance. It'll be your job to get your friends to tell good stories about them."

"Oh." Head bobbing in understanding, Jane grinned. "I'll get right on it."

"Good." Harry looked around the room. "Any questions?"

When no one answered, he gathered the file and his notes. "In that case, let's get to work."

After Jeb left, Kate turned to Jane. "It's your bedtime. Go get ready and I'll come kiss you."

"Can't I stay up a little longer?" Jane begged.

"It's a school night." Kate touched her daughter's hair with affection. "Besides, I have some things to discuss with Harry."

"Listen to your mother." Harry squeezed Jane's shoulder gently. "Be good. Go to bed."

"Okay." Jane rolled her eyes, as if to tell Kate that she was only doing what she asked because of Harry. "But I want Harry to tuck me in." She noticed the look on her mother's face. "It's client-attorney stuff."

Harry and Jane exchanged looks of co-conspirators. Kate's stomach tightened in response. Jane's hunger for a father's approval made her heart ache. As soon as possible, she needed to sit down with her daughter and discuss Roddy. Previously, she'd shied away from conversations, unable to think of Jane's father as anything less than Roddy-the-rat. Now, however, she could see Jane needed to know more. She sighed, knowing how difficult this conversation would be for them both.

"You go on up now. He'll be up in a little while, honey."

After Jane left, Kate opened the sliding glass doors to the wooden deck. "I think I need some fresh air."

After the warmth of the house, the cold air had bite.

Kate's breath showed clearly and then faded abruptly. Above, silver stars hung in an enormous black sky. She leaned against the railing and looked out at the surrounding trees, their outline a shade darker than the sky.

"Jane's a great kid. My brother's a jerk not to want to be in her life."

Kate had shared that view of Roddy for so long that it was hard to remember the good things about him. His zest for life, the bold, fearless way he rode, his charisma. She turned to face Harry. "Before we married, he told me he didn't want children." She could almost picture Roddy's handsome face carefully explaining how he wanted all of Kate's attention. "It was a deal-breaker, he said."

Harry stepped closer. "Are you telling me he's never even seen her?"

Kate shook her head. "The day I told him was the day he packed his bags. I waited six months for him to come to his senses." Her throat tightened at the memory of those long, lonely times. "I finally came home."

He covered her hands with his. "When I go back to Boston, I'll talk to him. Maybe if he saw a picture of Jane, he'd change his mind."

Kate laughed. "Right. I'm sure he and his future wife will joyfully embrace Jane." She shook her head. "You can try, but I wouldn't expect anything from him."

"Jane's beautiful," Harry said quietly. "Like her mother."

Harry's compliment pleased her. At the same time, Kate couldn't help but remember Roddy had, in fact, said the same thing about her looks. In time it had come to anger her. She'd wanted Roddy to see more than a pretty face. She wondered now if her desire to dig deeper into Roddy's character, and for him to do the same, had been as contributing a factor to the breakup of their marriage as her pregnancy.

"What were you thinking just then?"

She decided to be blunt. "About what you just said. Roddy used to tell me the same thing."

Harry leaned back against the railing, and for one horrible moment she wondered if the old wood would hold his weight. "I'm not Roddy."

Kate folded her arms around herself, although in truth, the coldness seemed unimportant. "But you're his brother. It's not that I'm not grateful for all your help. But before we go any farther, we'd better get something straight." She swallowed. "About what happened between us. I don't want . . ."

He held his hand up to stop her. "I don't expect anything from you, if that's what you were about to say."

"I know your time is valuable. I'll pay your fee." Kate drew a hand through her hair. Her fingers moved clumsily, rumpling rather that smoothing. "It'll take time, but you have my word."

"I don't want your money." Harry stuck his hands into the pockets of his jeans.

Silence fell between them. Kate watched the puffs of air come from his mouth and disappear into the night. Like him, she thought. After Monday he would leave without a trace. She swallowed with effort. "What is it then that you want?"

"Your mother's double chocolate brownies."

She laughed in relief. He'd looked so serious, and she'd been so afraid that he would want something she couldn't give.

"You got it." Kate lifted her gaze to meet his eyes. And then she felt something within her struggling. Her heart beat stronger, steadily accelerating, like a swan lifting wings long unused and fanning the water in preparation for flight.

Harry extended his hand to her. Kate's eyes dropped to his fingers, suddenly noticing in detail how beautiful they were, large and strong. Even before she extended her hand, she knew his grip would be warm.

She thought then that a kiss could seem like an unbreakable promise. A man's eyes could blaze with desire that he would call love, but wasn't. Even a man's words could ring with passion but lack truth. A man's touch, however, could not lie. She looked down at their joined hands, felt the bond between them, and wondered if it would be idiotic to believe in him.

"I'm not Roddy." Harry squeezed her hand. "I won't ever hurt you, Kate."

And then Jane banged on the glass behind them. There was the sound of her struggling with the heavy door and it finally heaving open. She slipped out onto the wooden deck, dancing joyfully in the night. Her thin, pink nightgown floated around her legs as she spun in the darkness, stopping to look up at them with a pleased, hopeful smile. "You didn't come up, so I came down." She fixed her gaze on Harry. "I'm ready for my tuck-in."

Kate smiled at the sight of her curly haired, beautiful child, who wanted nothing more than the deep sound of a male voice—a father's voice—to be the last thing she heard before she went to bed.

Harry drew back from her and tousled Jane's hair. "I'm going to tuck you in so tightly you won't be able to breathe."

Jane squealed in happy anticipation, sounding more like the little girl she was, and less like the teenager she'd been dressing like. She yelped with pleasure as Harry swept her up in his arms. The sound rang with such utter pleasure that Kate's heart ached for Jane; that this one simple act would be so precious. And her heart ached for both of them for what they missed.

Chapter Twelve

Could Harry pull off the defense? In the pale morning light, it seemed highly improbable. Yet, as Kate swept the stable aisle, she couldn't stop thinking about the strategy Harry had proposed the night before. Somehow he had infused them all with hope. She'd seen the light in her parents' faces. Up before dawn, they had tackled their assignments. Harry had even managed to make Jane feel important. Her daughter had scribbled pages of notes about the animals.

Returning the broom to the tack room, she nearly bumped into Maureen, who carried her saddle in her arms. "What are you doing here this early?

Maureen made a face. "What do you think?" She slipped a bridle higher over her shoulder. "I'm doing my assignment."

"It looks to me like you're going riding." Kate blocked her friend's path. "The injunction specifically states that no riding of any kind can take place on our land."

A smug expression crossed Maureen's features.

"I'm not going to be riding on your property." Her eyes gleamed. "I'm heading for the outskirts of Simon's golf course." She patted a thirty-five millimeter camera slung around her neck. "I'm going to check his fence line."

Kate crossed her arms across her chest. "Are you crazy?"

"Do you want to win this case?"

"Of course I do."

Maureen smiled. "Don't you see? If we can find something wrong with his fence line, then we can claim it's his fault your animals keep getting on his land.

This is scary, Kate thought. Maureen's idea actually made sense. She gazed at her friend with suspicion. "Why don't we just walk?"

"Because it's more fun to ride." Maureen looked hard at her friend. "Come on, Kate. We can cover more ground this way."

"I don't know. It's been a while since Raleigh's been ridden. You know how flaky he gets."

Maureen dismissed Kate's concerns with a wave of her hand. "You have to stop worrying so much. Come on, Kate, how long has it been since you've been on a horse?"

I should go with her, Kate decided, *just to keep Maureen out of trouble.*

About twenty minutes later, two horses clopped across Lake Street carrying the two women.

Despite her misgivings, Kate lifted her face to the morning sun. Maples and oaks lit the morning with warm red, yellow and orange leaves. Her spirits lifted with every step.

"Are you going to tell me what's going on? Ever

since that stakeout, you've been acting differently around Harry." Maureen tugged the reins as Raleigh, her horse, chomped a patch of leaves from a branch.

Kate tried not to smile. It had been impossible to think of anything since. She'd lain awake for the greater part of the night, both reliving the moment and promising herself not to repeat it. She didn't dare admit anything to Maureen. "You mean something besides nearly murdering Carla?"

Maureen's stirrup iron clanked against Kate's. "Come on, spill it."

"Keep your mind on business."

"Must be even better than I thought," Maureen chuckled as a blush appeared on Kate's face. "Tell me Auntie Maureen doesn't know a secret weapon when she sees one." She looked carefully at Kate. "I wasn't expecting you to fall for our legal weapon, though."

"Oh come on, Maureen." Kate carefully adjusted a strap on her saddle that didn't need adjusting. "Don't make more than what there is."

Kate studied the fence more in hope of avoiding Maureen's scrutiny than in finding a problem. Veering slightly off the trail, she pointed to the post and rail fence. "See those hoof prints? That's where Houdini jumped the fence."

Maureen tugged the reins, and her horse halted. She shot a few photos before dismounting and withdrawing a measuring tape. "Fifty inches," she proclaimed. "Darnit." She tapped her boot thoughtfully. "Maybe we could dig a little hole and measure again."

"Get real. Don't you think it's going to look slightly suspicious if I dig a trench under his fence?"

"Did I say trench? You can't be such a stickler for the rules, Kate. You're the only one who plays by them."

Kate gathered her reins. "Come on, Maureen. Let's get going. Honesty is supposed to be a good thing."

"Not when you're dealing with a slimeball like Simon." Maureen capped the camera lens. "People like him, they're leeches."

"It doesn't mean we have to be one too."

The horses moved forward again as Kate considered Maureen's words. A stickler for rules, a dependable person, the one who could be counted on to do the right thing. It wasn't the first time she had been called these things. Yet if she was different, who would everyone turn to?

She had never had the luxury of handing off her worries as if they were a heavy bag of groceries. What would it be like to have someone to share her problems with? What if that someone was Harry?

Kate stroked the muscular shoulder of her mare, admiring the way the sun brought out the copper highlights in her coat. "I don't always go by the rules."

"Are you kidding? The post office should create a stamp in your honor. You're a great daughter, a wonderful mother, and the best friend I'll ever have."

Kate smiled and moved her mare closer to Maureen's. Their legs bumped in a friendly sort of way. "Thanks, but I don't deserve the praise. You should have seen what I let Jane wear to school this morning. She had a paperclip glued to her belly button."

"You're kidding."

Kate gave a strangled laugh. "She twisted the paperclip to make it look like she pierced her belly button."

"Our Jane? Belly button piercing?" She slapped her thigh with satisfaction, which caused her horse to jump forward nervously. "I knew that girl had potential. When she's ready for the real thing, I'll have mine pierced too. How about you, Kate?"

"You're going to have to wait about twenty years before I allow any parts of her body to be pierced."

Maureen slapped a fly off her horse's neck. "She'll be teaching you the facts of life before you know it."

"I already know the facts of life thank you very much."

Maureen's mount swung his hindquarters to get a better look as a car sped down the road behind them.

"Yeah? Well, you have a hunky guy who's yours for the taking, and you don't even see it." Maureen pulled her reins as the tall, chestnut gelding snapped nervously at Kate's horse. "Even if he is related to that turd-brain Roddy."

"Which I haven't forgotten," Kate stated, as much for her own benefit as Maureen's.

Maureen laughed. "Maybe it's time you did." She gave Kate a pointed look. "He drools over you. Now, what are you going to do about it?"

"Nothing." Kate kept her eyes fixed on the trail. "Say thank you, when he leaves." She paused. "Because he will leave. Men are good at that."

"Oh, get over it. Just because you let one guy break your heart, don't think all guys are like that."

"Easy for you to say." Kate shot Maureen a sideways glance. "You have Jimmy. He adores you."

"Doesn't mean we'll have a happy ending," Maureen pointed out. "The divorce is still very much in question." She narrowed her eyes. "Something is happening between you and Harry. I just know it."

"Will you quit it?" Kate nudged her horse faster. "I've known him less than a week."

"A day, a week, a hundred years. When two souls connect, there's love."

They rode in silence as Kate considered Maureen's words. "Don't you think I have enough complications in my life right now without adding a man to them?"

"He's not a complication, Kate. He's going to save you from yourself, if you don't kill him off first."

A squirrel raced ahead of them on the path. Raleigh shied sideways. Even Kate's mare stiffened. "Easy, girl." She stroked the mare's coat absently. "Harry drools over me?"

"He's a complete mush."

Kate straightened in the saddle. "Describe mush."

"Mush is playing bodyguard to a horse, tearing down a building practically with his bare hands, and now organizing your defense."

"So, if you were me, what would you do?" It occurred to Kate that asking Maureen's advice about men probably wasn't a great idea.

"I'd go for it, Kate. Let nature take its course."

"Maureen, would you be serious? This time, it's got to be the real thing. The whole nine yards. I want the happily-ever-after."

"Okay, get Harry on a horse and try galloping off into the sunset with him." She cocked a thin, arched brow. "That's a happily-ever-after ending, right? Of course, since the sun sets in the west, you'll have to ride across Simon's golf course." She paused. "He'd probably shoot you, if he catches you, which means I'll have to shoot him, which is not a happily-ever-after type of ending."

"Thanks, Maureen, for those words of encouragement."

Maureen laughed. "I can't tell you what to do. However, I suggest you stop blushing and get aggressive."

"I don't blush." Kate straightened in the saddle. "I windburn easily."

Maureen snorted with laughter, which caused her horse to shy nervously. "Funny, you haven't had a problem with the wind in the nearly thirty years I've known you." She pulled the reins to slow Raleigh's jig. "Seduce him. I'll help. If things don't go well, we'll handcuff him."

Before she could help herself, Kate imagined Harry's large wrists and discovered that she found his wrists as appealing as anything else about him. "I can't."

"So you're just going to let Harry walk away without even fighting for him?"

Kate looked straight at the post and rail fence, which so far did not even show a crack. "When a man wants to leave, generally speaking, he leaves and doesn't look back."

Maureen touched her arm. "And when men want to stay, they find a way, even if it doesn't make sense to anyone." She smiled almost apologetically. "He looks at you sometimes, Kate, with this expression I can't even begin to describe, but it makes me lose my breath."

Urging her horse into a trot, Kate moved ahead. She didn't want to hear any platitudes about love. Maureen wasn't the one who would have to pick up the pieces when Harry left. Kate knew only too well that love and desire were two faces of the same coin. She had no need to flip that coin and see what fate would do to her life again.

The path turned to the left and up a short hill. Dead leaves made the incline slippery, and Kate leaned forward to help her mare balance. The mare attacked the hill, ascending in a series of jumps that sent loose dirt, rocks and leaves rolling backwards. Behind her, she heard Maureen's horse scrambling up the hill with her friend crouched over his neck.

At the top of the hill, Kate pulled the reins. She gestured with her arm. "We should measure the fence line here."

Maureen's horse sidestepped nervously. He'd spied a rabbit crouched by the path and did not want to walk past it. Maureen nudged the reluctant horse, who swung his hindquarters into Kate's mare, who pinned her ears.

"Easy, girl." Kate steadied her mare.

Maureen's face puckered in concentration. Her hands raised nervously on the reins, sending her horse's head skyward and brought him to an uneasy stop. In her desire to correct the horse, Maureen over-compensated and her horse stepped backward.

"Stop it." Maureen jerked the reins.

There was a sudden loud crunching noise as the big roan's hindquarters hit the fence. To Kate's amazement, when the horse felt the fence press against his hindquarters, he began to sit.

"Kate!" Maureen yelled as the pitch of her horse's back nearly toppled her over backward.

Kate grabbed for the reins, but it was too late. The fence gave way with a loud, cracking noise, as if an oak had fallen.

Holding tightly to the reins, Kate moved her mare forward. For a moment, Raleigh's neck stretched but his buttocks remained on the ground.

"Get up you knucklehead!" Maureen shouted.

Grunting, the horse leaped to his feet, all but unseating Maureen as he surged forward.

"Oh no." Kate released the roan's bridle and stared at the squashed fence. *What am I going to tell Harry?*

She looked around nervously, half-expecting someone to have seen them.

Maureen spiked her short blond hair, which was already standing on end. "Oh boy."

"Oh boy is right," Kate said. "What are we going to do?"

Kate and Maureen exchanged worried glances. They looked again at the scattered poles cut as neatly as if a kung fu master had taken his hand to them.

"Kate, I'm so sorry." She raked her fingers through her hair. "I can't believe this happened."

Kate shook her head. It wasn't all Maureen's fault. She never should have agreed to her friend's plan. "Don't worry, Maureen. We'll fix it." She meant that somehow things would work out, and Maureen was not to feel badly. Maureen, however, took her literally.

"No, Kate. I'll fix the fence. You stay out of this one."

"No way, Maureen. I meant we'd work it out, legally. Not fix the fence ourselves." She gave her friend a strict look.

"If that creep Simon finds out what happened, you might as well kiss the stable good-bye," Maureen said bluntly. "Look, I'm a policewoman. I know the law better than you do, but in some cases the justice system works best when you bend the rules." She frowned at Kate. "All I'll be doing is helping out a neighbor without his knowing it."

It was more than that. Kate chewed her lip thoughtfully. While she didn't like concealing what they'd done, in a way it made sense. Simon would get his fence fixed and the stable would stay out of trouble.

She met Maureen's gaze. "Okay, but I'm not letting you do this by yourself." She shortened her reins and turned the mare around. "Besides, it's going to take both of us to carry the new poles."

Maureen's gaze locked with Kate's. "I should do this by myself. It'll be a lot worse if you're caught."

"Then we won't get caught." Kate urged her mare down the incline. "We'll do it tonight, when it gets dark. We've just got to hope that nobody notices the fence until we have a chance to come back and fix it." She raised her hand when her friend started to protest. "Agreed?"

After a moment Maureen nodded. "Agreed." She urged Raleigh after Kate's horse. "Sorry about the fence, Kate."

"Don't worry about it; it can be fixed." And she thought about things that could not be as easily fixed, like broken hearts and broken dreams.

Chapter Thirteen

Leaning against the weathered side of the barn, Harry watched the two riders cross the street. He heard giggling and saw Kate and Maureen exchange looks. *What have they been up to?*

He didn't have to wait long to find out. The riders soon pulled up in front of him. His eyes narrowed at the guilt stamped across both faces. "I thought you weren't supposed to be riding."

"You assigned me to Simon. We needed to see if Simon's fence line met code," Maureen answered for Kate, who seemed fascinated by the pommel of her saddle.

"Was it?"

"It *was*." Maureen shot another look at Kate, who had turned a dark shade of red.

What is going on? Harry feared the worst. "What did you two do now?"

"We didn't do anything." Maureen's voice rang with false innocence. "Right, Kate?"

A smile flashed across Kate's face and then disappeared. "Right."

"Then why are you two giggling?"

"No reason." Maureen dismounted with a thump beside Harry. "Can't two women have a nice ride together without something happening?"

"Maybe, but not *you* two." Harry looked hard at Maureen. "You didn't trample anyone, did you?" He hoped that Simon wasn't dead and buried in a sand trap. However, as he looked at Kate, he knew he was prepared to defend her if she had.

"We didn't do anything to Simon." Maureen loosened Raleigh's girth. "Although that's not a bad idea."

Harry fixed his gaze on Kate. "Tell me what's so funny."

His hand slid to her shoulder. Beneath her soft chambray shirt he felt the curve of muscle, the solidness of bone. He looked down at her faint dusting of freckles across her nose and brick-red cheeks. Without thinking, Harry tested the heat of her skin with his finger. "What happened?" The command was softened by the lightness of his touch.

"Raleigh sat on Simon's fence and broke it."

Harry's head jerked back. "What?"

"He backed into it and sat down. The fence couldn't hold him."

Harry eyed the broad hindquarters of the horse with respect. "He broke the fence?"

"Yep." Maureen patted her horse's neck. "The fence obviously was old and fragile. Just waiting for—"

"—a horse to come along and sit on it." Harry raked his fingers through his hair. "This is not going to win points with the judge. Simon will use this against you."

"Well, Simon's not going to know," Kate said matter-of-factly.

"We're going to fix the fence," Maureen finished.

Harry looked from one woman to the other. "You're just going to walk across the street carrying a couple of eight-foot poles and no one's going to notice?"

Kate shifted her weight under his scrutiny. "We'll wait until it gets dark."

Harry folded his arms across his chest. "You could be arrested for trespassing."

"I'll bring my badge," Maureen said. "If someone stops us, I'll say we're on police business."

"While carrying fence poles across a golf course in the middle of the night?" Harry shook his head. "I don't think so."

"What should we do?" Kate asked. "I can't leave the fence broken. Sooner or later someone will see it."

Harry sighed. "We'll fix the fence tonight." He stared at Maureen hard. "You're staying. I'm going."

"But—"

"But what?"

"I'm the best person for a covert operation."

"Maureen, I hate to agree with Harry, but he's right. If you're caught, it could cost you your job."

Maureen stuck her thumb at Harry. "What about *his* job?"

"I won't get caught." Harry hoped this was true. "Which is not what I can say for you and Kate. You two are the equestrian equivalents of Thelma and Louise."

Kate and Maureen exchanged guilty smiles.

"It's settled then," Harry said. "Kate and I will fix the fence tonight."

"Okay." Maureen slipped the reins over Raleigh's

head and led the horse into the barn. "But take a walkie-talkie. I'll stake out Simon's house tonight. His house is near the broken fence and if he decides to go for a walk, I'll warn you."

As Maureen towed her horse into the barn, Harry stuck his hands into the pocket of his jeans. "What is it about you and fences?"

Shrugging, Kate tilted her head to look up at him. "It was an accident, Harry. There wasn't much room, and when Raleigh got startled . . ."

"I've been here less than a week. So far, I've seen two fences, one building and a middle-aged woman go down."

Smiling, Kate met his gaze. She brushed a mass of coarse brown forelock out of her mare's eyes. "At least you can say we're not boring."

Her words touched a chord within him. He might love the law, but if he were honest, Harry had had more than his share of boring clients. Some of the people he'd defended looked at him with less expression than the horse standing in front of him. In fact, as the horse thrust its head toward him, Harry felt certain it was trying to communicate with him. "What does it want?"

"Her ears rubbed."

Under Harry's fingers, the horse's ear felt surprisingly silky and warm. The horse lowered its head even further to give him better access.

If anyone had told him three days ago that he would be massaging a horse's ear, he'd have laughed in their face. However, reflected into the mare's luminous brown eye, he saw himself; a thirty-four-year-old man with a morning's worth of stubble and a shine in his eyes that hadn't been there in quite a while.

The horse sighed blissfully onto his shirt. The warm air tickled. Harry wondered who was enjoying this more—himself or the horse. "She's not going to OD on this, is she? We're not going to have to add a dead horse to the list, are we?"

Kate laughed. The sound made him catch his breath. Knowing he was responsible for inspiring that rich, beautiful sound filled him with as much pleasure as any court case he could remember winning.

He'd always prided himself on his ability to read people. Their expressions of fear, greed, insecurity, and even, at times, insanity, had looked back at him more often than he cared to admit. Yet, he knew that these glimpses into people's lives were only that. Some of this superficiality had carried over into his personal life, he realized. He hadn't wanted the women he dated to look too deeply into his character, and he hadn't been too interested in theirs. He hadn't wanted more.

For the first time he wondered if this was enough; if the view from the life he'd worked so hard to attain was half as beautiful as the sweeping hills and grassy meadows around him.

Chapter Fourteen

Kate stuck her hands in her pockets and shivered. The air felt heavy as if any minute it would rain. Through the beam of Harry's flashlight she saw bony roots of trees protruding through the slick coat of brown pine needles. She shot him a sideways look. "The best poles are on top of the extra wood from the lean-to."

Harry's backpack clanked lightly as they descended the trail. "You're sure they're the right size and length?"

"It's a standard size." Kate looked up at the threatening dark sky. "It's going to rain."

As if her words opened some kind of heavenly spout, the first drops of rain splattered Kate's upturned face. They were cold and promised to soak her to the bone.

"At least there's no lightning."

The beam of Harry's flashlight highlighted the pile of poles rolled loosely on top of each other.

Harry swung a pole up on his shoulder, easily shouldering its weight. Kate selected a pole and lifted. Underneath, a family of mice streamed out. They spilled over the sides of the remaining poles. One scrambled over the top of Kate's boot. She shrieked.

Harry, who had been practicing various ways of balancing the heavy pole on his shoulders, nearly lost his footing at the sound of Kate's scream. Dropping the pole, he ran to her side just in time to see the last brown mouse disappear. He laughed.

Kate glared at him. "You're laughing."

"You're supposed to be such a nature girl. Instead, you're scared of a little mouse."

Kate narrowed her eyes. "Not a mouse. Mice. There was a herd of them." She shuddered. "They bite, you know."

"They're more afraid of us than we are of them." Harry aimed the beam at the woodpile. "Besides, mice don't travel in herds." He grinned. "Mice have families, nice, friendly families."

"Not these mice." Kate reached for the fence pole that Harry had dropped. She balanced it over one shoulder. "Seeing that you're so brave, I guess you won't mind picking up another pole."

Harry shrugged. Reaching down, he lifted a beam. "Nothing to it." Swinging the wood to his shoulder, he faced Kate.

"Harry." Kate's eyes were huge. "There's a . . ."

"Don't even try it."

"But there's a . . ."

Before she could get a word out, a large spider scurried the length of the pole and climbed onto Harry's hand.

Harry screamed and threw the pole down. He shook himself wildly to the laughter and delight of Kate.

"What's the matter, Harry? It's only a little spider. It's much more afraid of you than you are of it."

Continuing to brush his arms, Harry shook his head. "You could have warned me."

"I tried."

Growling, Harry checked the pole.

"I think the spiders are long gone," Kate offered innocently. "I've never heard any person scream so loudly in my life."

Harry paused to glare at her before shouldering the fence pole for the second time.

"On to Simon's," Kate called gaily and turned.

Harry ducked as Kate's pole barely missed his head. "Hey, you nearly decapitated me."

"What?" Kate turned around, nearly whacking him in the head again.

"You're as dangerous with that pole as you are with tools."

"I am not, Harry. It's the rain making everything so slippery."

Maureen's voice squawked from Kate's back pocket. "Jade, this is Zephyr. Come in. Come in."

"Jade? Zephyr? You two have *code* names?"

Kate nearly dropped the pole reaching for the walkie-talkie. "These are police-quality radios. Maureen thought we should have aliases in case someone else tapped into our frequency. You have a code name as well. It's Eagle." She managed to wedge the black radio between her ear and shoulder. "This is Jade."

"I'm at the subject's house." Maureen's voice carried clearly through the rain to Harry. "Why does a scumbag like him get to live in a mansion? He's got an awesome view of the fifth hole."

"Do you see him, Maur, er, Zephyr?"

"Ten-four. He's got the curtains wide open. I'm going in for a closer look."

"Be careful."

"Don't worry," Maureen assured her. "I was born for nights like this."

"I mean it, Zephyr. Don't take any chances."

"I won't." There was a brief pause. "But that doesn't mean *you* can't."

Even in the darkness Kate felt herself blush. She replaced the walkie-talkie. "She's talking about fixing the fence. That we should risk getting caught. That's what she meant by taking chances."

Kate heard herself rambling. Maureen had meant something else entirely. She just hoped Harry wouldn't catch on.

The rain increased, blurring their vision and filling their ears with the sound of pattering leaves. Kate tripped over a rock in the path. The pole flew out of her hands and banged on the ground.

A few steps behind, Harry called, "You okay?"

"Yes, but look out for that rock."

"What rock?" Harry's boot hit something solid. He lurched, barely managing to keep his grip on the pole.

Kate laughed. "That rock."

"We need one of those miner's hats," Harry grumbled, shifting the weight of the pole to his other shoulder.

"I thought the moon would be out."

"I'm glad it isn't," Harry replied. "We don't want to be seen. This isn't exactly something that I want to add to my resume."

It rained harder then, soaking Kate's hair, shoulders, and sliding coldly into her eyes, which she couldn't wipe without risk of losing her grip on the pole.

On foot, the path seemed longer, the terrain more difficult than Kate remembered. Her shoulder ached from the weight of the pole, and by the time they got to the last, steep pitch, even breathing required more energy than she had.

"Almost there." Kate's hair lay plastered to her skull, and rain dripped down her cheeks. She turned her head and could not see Harry's large, dark shape behind her. Her ears heard nothing. "Harry?"

"What?"

The one word managed to convey a wealth of discomfort and hostility.

"Nothing." She paused. "Just wanted to make sure you were still there."

"I'm still here. Are we hiking to Canada or is the end in sight?"

"Just up this hill." Kate drew a deep breath. It's pretty steep, and there are pine needles on the ground, so be careful."

Kate adjusted the pole on her shoulder, bent forward and began to climb. The leather bottoms on her boots fought for traction on the wet pine needles, and her posture tipped so far forward she smelled the wet earth. She took two steps and slid backwards.

Harry stepped to the side as she landed near his feet. Looking down at her, he said, "You'd make a great bowling ball, Kate."

Kate glared up at Harry, blinking back the rain. "You try it if it looks so easy."

Harry eyed the black pitch in front of him. "Piece of cake. All you need to know is where to put your feet."

Striding past Kate, he put momentum into his effort and had ascended half the hill before his feet lost traction. He scrambled madly, but a few moments later, ended up next to Kate.

Kate laughed. "Guess you didn't know where to put your feet."

Harry grumbled. "We're going to have to do this together." He handed her one end of his pole. "You take the front. I'll push."

With Harry holding much of the weight of the pole, Kate climbed more easily. Before she'd climbed halfway up the hill, she found herself using both hands and knees to pull herself upward. The pole balanced over her shoulder, occasionally bumping her neck.

When Kate reached the top, she let the pole drop to the ground and shouted in victory. Somewhere, a dog barked in response.

"What are you trying to do, Kate, wake the entire neighborhood?"

Her jeans were covered with mud, her sweatshirt was soaked, and her hair lay plastered to her head, and she didn't care. Kate extended her hand to Harry, pulling him over the lip of the hill. "We did it."

His hair, black and unruly, glistened on his head. Rain streamed down his face. His glasses had fogged. In the moonless night, she could barely make out the dark slash of his mouth. His eyes, infinitely darker than the night, reflected such intensity that Kate forgot about their mission, about the rain, about his relationship to the man who had once broken her heart.

The angle of her neck produced a small gap in her sweatshirt, which the rain quickly found. Icy droplets crawled down Kate's front. The thighs of her jeans stuck to her legs, effectively shrink-wrapping them. Her discomfort, however, came not from the weather but from an ache deep inside.

Harry's arms wrapped around her so tightly that her breath left her in one big gasp. His face bent to hers, all at once familiar and dear. That he would kiss her here, in the woods, beneath the blanket of night seemed not only fitting, but right.

His lips felt cold but warmed quickly. He tasted of rain and something as deep and basic as the old oaks and pines surrounding them. Kate pressed her body tightly against his, blurring the lines of their bodies until the last spaces between them disappeared. Harry deepened the kiss, holding nothing back. Kate could feel his strength and heat flowing through her body, driving out the last vestiges of hurt and pain that had been Roddy's legacy, and the lingering doubts that she would ever feel anything too deeply for a man again.

Distantly, just beyond the drumming of the rain, Kate registered the sound of dogs barking urgently. *Let them bark all they want*, Kate thought. *Let the lights come on in every house within ten miles.* She didn't need them to warn her. She knew the dangers of kissing someone like this, holding nothing back and giving everything she had.

Harry's breath came in short, hard puffs and his hands clenched so tightly around her shoulders it hurt. Her body was warm where it touched him. Her hands tugged at his neck and she reached higher on her tip-toes.

Every muscle in Harry's body had gone rigid. He could have been carved from marble. His physical strength awed her, but at the same time, like her, he seemed oddly vulnerable.

"Kate." His voice, low and deep, gave her an electric charge.

She wanted to stand there forever—letting the rain

pound down—safe within the shield of his body. She'd never believed that a person's life could be circular, that a person could find herself at the place where everything had started. Yet here she was, falling for Harry in a way she had never imagined.

A voice blurted through the darkness. "Jade, come in."

Maureen again. Kate wanted to turn off the radio. Better yet, throw it into the woods. Let Maureen have a nice conversation with the squirrels.

"Jade, are you there?"

Harry nuzzled her ear. "Tell her you're busy." He reached for the radio. "I'll tell her."

"Zephyr this is Eagle," he said. "We've reached the target area. We can't talk right now. Repeat, we can't talk right now."

"Well, you should see Simon right now." Kate couldn't help but grin at the glee in her friend's voice. "He's getting ready for bed, and he's wearing green briefs with little white golf balls on them." The radio crackled. "The way he looks in them should be a crime." Suddenly Kate heard a banging noise. "Oops," Maureen said after a moment. "I slipped against the window. I don't think he noticed, though, he was too busy flexing his muscles in front of the mirror. Over and out."

Harry replaced the radio.

"Eagle?" Kate touched the rain on his cheek.

Harry laughed. "Yes, Jade?"

"We'd better fix the fence."

The wind sheeted through the trees, sending a fresh wave of water spraying over them. The rain on her lips tasted like Harry.

"Okay." His arms reluctantly released her.

Together they walked to the broken fence. Harry tossed a piece of broken pole into the edge of the woods. He shook the post with his hands.

"Don't tell me the post needs re-setting." Kate wiped the rain off her face.

"It's fine."

"Then let's finish and get out of here."

Picking up a fence pole, Kate dragged it to the post. Harry stepped close to help her fit it into the fence. For a moment their hands touched. Kate turned to smile into Harry's eyes and found herself blinded by the beam of a high-powered flashlight.

"Police!" a male voice rang out of the darkness. "Freeze!"

Kate spun around as a tall policeman dressed in rain gear stepped into view.

Wiping her cold, wet face with equally cold, wet hands, Kate stared in horror at the policeman. She squinted against the light in her eyes. Did he actually have a gun pointed at them?

"Put your hands up," the officer ordered, "and step away from the fence."

"Officer, we can explain." Harry raised his hands.

The policeman stepped closer. "It looks pretty clear to me. You're vandalizing the fence."

"We weren't vandalizing the fence," Kate cried. "We were fixing it."

"You can explain it to the judge," the officer said. "I'm sure you have an explanation, too, for spying into the home of Mr. Simon Trebeck." He looked them over. "He called to tell us he had a peeper."

Simon had spotted Maureen after all. Kate felt like smacking herself in the head. She and Harry should have abandoned the plan immediately after Maureen had slipped against the window.

"Keep your hands up."

The officer meant to pat them down. Instinctively, Kate stepped closer to Harry. "This is a misunderstanding," Harry said.

"Sure," the officer said, "you two are just good Samaritans out on a rainy night fixing people's fences." He laughed. "If you're so innocent, why the code names? I picked up your transmissions on the radio, Eagle." He pointed the flashlight's beam to the path behind them. "Let's go."

"Officer, wait," Kate cried. "The truth is that I broke the fence this afternoon and didn't want to tell anyone."

The officer ran his flashlight over Kate. "You broke this fence all by yourself?"

"Actually a horse sat on it."

"You mean elephant, right?" The officer snorted. "Do I look like an idiot?" He held the beam on Kate's face a moment longer. "Wait a minute. I recognize you." He swung the beam over Harry. "You're the barn people. You own the horse that clocked that woman last night." He paused. "I don't know what's going on here, but we better go back to the station."

On the way to the police station, Kate and Harry sat next to each other in the back seat of the patrol car. As the car roared down the highway, Kate watched the lights stream by. Harry hadn't said a word since they'd handcuffed him.

"Look on the bright side of things." Kate sounded to her own ears exactly like her mother. "At least we're not going to have to call a lawyer."

Harry didn't smile.

"Say something," she ordered. "What are you thinking?"

He turned toward her. "I'm planning our defense. It's going to be complicated, considering we're facing charges for vandalism and voyeurism. Frankly, I'm considering pleading insanity."

"I'm sorry you got dragged into this, Harry." She wiggled a fraction closer to him. "We'll get everything straightened out." When Harry remained silent, she added, "I'm sure that Maureen can explain everything."

Turning, Harry met her gaze. "Maureen is going to straighten this out? In that case, we're definitely pleading guilty by reason of insanity."

Chapter Fifteen

"Uncle Harry? What are you doing?" Jane's boots clumped on the wooden floor as she crossed the office to peer over Harry's shoulder.

Harry looked up from the desk. He tried not to stare at his niece's purple lipstick and metallic-gold eyeshadow. "Legal stuff."

Jane dragged a three-legged stool closer to Harry. "Is my mother going to jail?"

"No." He smiled at her. "Your Aunt Maureen explained everything." In truth, for a while there, it had been touch and go. There'd even been an awful moment when he'd considered whom he would call to make bail.

Jane looked at him with huge eyes. "I might be a lawyer when I grow up. Horse people need a lot of defending."

"They certainly do."

"Actually, kids do too." Jane curled a strand of hair around her finger. "I told my friends about you. Everyone wants to hire you in case they don't get into the club."

Harry frowned. "Your friends want a lawyer?"

"We believe it's called a class action suit."

Harry simply stared at her. First, a restraining order on behalf of a quarter horse, and now representing a group of girls who hadn't been invited into a club. He'd be representing the Guinea hens next if he wasn't careful. It was on the tip of Harry's tongue to point out that he'd agreed to help Jane, not her friends, when the comment died on his lips.

"What kind of club is so important?"

Harry was rewarded by a look of relief. Jane lowered her voice although they were alone.

"It's called the kissing boys club. Once you've kissed a boy, you get to belong." She lifted her chin. "I'm pretty close to joining, but a couple of my friends, well, unless we all help, there's no way."

"We're talking about a kiss on the cheeks?" Harry asked hopefully.

Jane's cheeks turned tomato red. "Lips only. Extra points if you—"

"How old are you?" Harry interrupted.

"Ten."

For a moment he considered filing blanket restraining orders on any boy who came within one hundred yards of her. And, if anyone broke it, he'd bury that boy in a blizzard of legal paperwork. He was a lawyer and knew how to do it. And then it occurred to him that he might be having some sort of pre-middle-aged crisis to be writing restraining orders to protect horses, and now fantasizing about fatherhood.

"I think you should talk to your mother about this," Harry said.

Jane rolled her eyes. "My mother is very conservative when it comes to things like this."

"Is she?"

"Oh yes. She never dates."

"Never?" Keeping his tone casual, Harry forced his features into a neutral expression that hung on his face as uncomfortably as lopsided curtains.

Jane shrugged. "She went out with the veterinarian a few times because Aunt Maureen made her, but that stopped after she gave him a black eye."

Harry grinned and leaned back, catching himself just before the chair toppled over. Outside the window, he caught a glimpse of Kate walking toward the pasture with some hay in her arms. Could the woman even breathe in those tight jeans?

He flashed back to earlier that morning when he'd found Kate in the stable aisle grooming a large brown horse. Before he'd known it, she'd put a brush in his hand.

"You go with the coat, not against it," she'd explained.

At first he'd moved uncertainly, afraid of hurting the horse if he brushed too vigorously. Kate, then, had placed her fingers over his on the brush and guided his fingers.

"This is the crest of her neck." Sliding his hand down the creamy slope of hair and muscle, Kate began to teach him how horses were made. "It leads to her withers."

Wordlessly, their hands had moved over the horse's body, tracing the swirl of hair forming over the mare's hip bone, dipping into the soft, fine folds of skin behind her front legs. His fingers burned with sensation, and Harry knew he could never look at a horse again without remembering the extraordinary sensation of Kate's hand, teaching his to see.

The horse was velvet and bone, smooth muscle, and warm hair.

When she finished, she released Harry's hand and the sudden coolness where her hand had been made him aware how precious the contact had been. He'd stood there, a man who built his career on the intimate knowledge of the English language, completely speechless. Filled with wonder, long seconds had passed as he grinned at Kate, unable to take his gaze off her, unable to stop himself from reaching for her, and unable to believe this was anything but love.

"Harry?"

"Yes, Jane?"

"Your butt is ringing."

"Yes, her butt is," Harry stopped himself. With his gaze still on Kate, he handed the phone to Jane. "You take it."

Jane giggled. "Hello." She held the phone out to Harry. "It's for you."

"Take a message." Harry had a pretty good idea who was calling.

"He's busy. Call back," Jane's voice was packed full of importance. "Jane," she added. "Jane Withers," she said after a moment's pause. And then, with dignity, "Who are you?" Pause. "You're going to have to call back. He's busy. Suing someone's butt, I believe."

Harry tried not to laugh. Jane sat straighter in the seat. "I can't tell you that. It's part of a de-clothing thing."

Jane held the phone out to Harry. "He wants to talk to you."

Harry reached for the phone. He wasn't smiling

when he hung up a few minutes later. His colleague hadn't been amused or charmed by Jane, nor had he been supportive of Harry's delay. There'd been an un-expected development in the Corning versus Myers case. Corning was one of their most important clients, and usually Harry handled everything personally.

Jane regarded him with a knowing look. "You're supposed to be in Boston, aren't you?"

"Yup."

"I should have taken a message." She twisted her long hair around her hand. "When do you leave?"

Trust Jane to cut right to the chase. Harry folded his hands in his lap. He had his father's business wait-ing for him in Boston and a life most lawyers only dreamed about. Why put his plans in jeopardy?

The answer walked back into sight. Her long hair, swept back in a ponytail, cascaded down the straight, proud length of her spine. Kate needed him. Others too. Jane, Prissy, Harlan, Jimmy, and Maureen. He realized he hadn't answered Jane's question. "I don't know."

"Before you go," Jane said slowly, "could you teach me some more legal phrases?" Her eyes grew round and solemn. "I might need them on Monday when we go to court."

Harry sighed. The sound could have been produced by the sudden ache in his heart. The tilt of her jaw told him that Jane, indeed, would not hesitate to help her mother defend the stable.

"Have I told you lately that you're going to make quite a lawyer someday? Just warn me when you get your bar card because I sure don't want to oppose you in court."

* * *

Kate's heart raced. Okay, she told herself, she'd kissed him twice. So what? Kissing someone wasn't a crime. It didn't have to mean anything either. She could pretend it hadn't happened. Put it down to the heat of the moment, a momentary lapse of common-sense. Never mind what happened this morning when she'd gone temporarily insane and tried to teach Harry how to groom a horse. She'd been the one who'd ended up learning just how little control she had of her feelings when it came to Harry. *Okay, I can't trust myself around him, so what now?*

Complete avoidance, self-denial, and if all else fails run like crazy. Wait a minute. That's what I've been doing for the past nine years. Maybe I should trust my heart? Isn't that what faith is all about anyway?

"Kate?"

She jumped at the sound of Harry's voice. Her gaze darted about for a good hiding spot. In a moment of self-pity, she decided Harry wouldn't be content until he'd penetrated every layer of defense she had. He'd return to Boston only after he'd assured himself he'd truly broken her heart.

She looked around the barn, at the friendly faces of the horses watching her. They nickered at the sound of Harry's voice, again calling her name.

With only seconds remaining, Kate bolted for the ladder to the loft. Rushing in her haste to escape detection, Kate's boots slipped on the rusty rung of the ladder. She would have fallen if her hands hadn't grabbed a rung at the last moment. Her heart stopped when Harry's voice came from directly below her. "Kate?"

She rested her cheek against the cool rung. Busted. *Whatever you do*, she promised herself, *don't talk about anything personal. Keep the conversation general and keep moving. Above all, be calm.* "I'm throwing down hay for the evening feeding, Harry." Was it her imagination or did her voice sound like she'd swallowed helium?

"I've been looking for you."

She pulled herself up the last rung and into the relative safety of the loft. "Well, I guess you found me."

"I was just talking to Jane. There's something we need to talk about."

She released her breath slowly. *Good.* He probably didn't want to talk about where they had left off either. "You don't have to tell me. The school called this morning." Kate sat back on her heels. "I'll talk to her about the dress code."

She hoped he'd leave her alone, but to her dismay, he followed her into the loft. Light spilled from a single bulb, which illuminated golden bales of hay and cast shadows in the corners. Kate inhaled the thick aroma of the pungent hay and thought that even the scent of the place was dangerous, reeking of sun, and freshly plowed fields.

"You know about Jane?" Harry asked.

She wondered why he seemed surprised. "She wasn't the only girl who dressed inappropriately." Her eyes deliberately avoided his gaze. "By the way, I called Uncle Jeb about what happened last night on the golf course. He's called an emergency meeting."

To her relief, Harry stepped back. "I talked to him too. After what happened last night, he's more convinced than ever we need to prepare for the worst."

"I know." Kate dragged a bale toward a gap in the floor and kicked it through the hole. "If he weren't family, he'd quit the case."

"Is he always so pessimistic?"

As Kate reached for another bale, Harry hurried to help. She ground her teeth together as their shoulders touched. "As a matter of fact, yes. He has all the optimism of the captain of the *Titanic*."

Chuckling, Harry dropped a bale through the opening. He reached for another, handling the bulky hay easily. "I had an uncle like him."

Kate shot a quick look at his profile. What uncle? Roddy certainly hadn't mentioned anyone like Jeb. Then again, Roddy had been particularly fond of talking about Roddy. She wondered about Harry's other childhood memories, about his friends, about his life in Boston.

Remember, Kate, curiosity is a dangerous thing. If only a part of her would stop hoping this time it would be different. That the spark between she and Harry would blaze into something real and lasting.

She turned her back on him and reminded herself not to talk about what had happened between them last night, and then proceeded to do exactly that. "We need to talk about last night," she said.

"I thought it was rather straightforward," Harry replied. "Simon caught Maureen spying on him and called the cops. The policeman saw our flashlights and assumed it was us."

"I meant the kiss." Sweat as prickly as hay poked through her skin.

"Oh." His voice lowered.

For Pete's sake, what was wrong with her? What good could be gained by talking about something she shouldn't have let happen? She walked to the open window where the rope swing hung from the old oak tree. She and Maureen had spent many happy hours sailing through the air and landing in the soft, golden hay below.

Jane played on the swing just like she had so many years ago. Absently, Kate wondered if it would still hold her weight. Looking at the swing, she thought suddenly of her marriage, of all the weight she had made it bear. She'd wanted too much from Roddy. She'd expected him to take Maureen's place as a friend, and give her the same, unconditional love her parents gave her. No wonder the marriage had failed.

She didn't turn around, not even when Harry came up behind her. If she looked at him, it would be so easy to forget the reality of their situation and succumb to the longing, to the ceaseless ache of a heart that believed in lasting, romantic love, and even worse, believed in Harry. "Whatever we have between us is getting out of control."

Harry's voice rumbled dangerously close to her ear. "Maybe we've both tried to be in control for too long."

Shaking her head, Kate drew her fingers through her hair. "I can't do this." She turned slowly, longing for him to understand. "I can't think about you right now. About us." Her gaze searched his face. "My focus has to be the stable right now."

Harry frowned. "We can work on your court case and have feelings for each other."

"When Monday comes, Harry, what will happen? Will you get in your Explorer and drive off into the sunset?"

A muscle in Harry's cheek twitched, but he didn't answer her questions. "I thought so, Harry." She lifted her chin a fraction. "I'm glad we can be honest with each other."

"Kate," Harry said gently, "we haven't had time to

figure out the future, or even what we mean to each other right now."

Kate's eyes closed at the emotion evident in Harry's voice. Part of her wanted to throw caution to the wind and ask what he *thought* she meant to him. Commonsense insisted she let the opportunity pass.

"It's not every client that I'd risk going to jail for." Harry's voice had taken on a soft, teasing quality that Kate found difficult to resist.

"You may be a risk-taker, Harry, but I'm not. Not anymore."

"Are you still in love with him?" Harry's lips hardly moved at all. "With Roddy?"

Kate would have laughed, but she saw how important her answer was to him. "No. I don't think I ever was." She thought for a moment. "I was too busy trying to get him to love me."

Harry tucked a strand of Kate's hair behind her ear. "How could he possibly not have loved you?"

She felt something easing within her. "I was pretty young, and had all these great expectations for what love could be."

His finger trailed the curve of her ear. "But all these years, are you sure you haven't been carrying a torch for Roddy?"

It touched her to see the trace of doubt in his eyes. "Roddy was the first boy who asked me out." She felt shy and embarrassed and wondered why she seemed bent on baring her past to him. "He made me feel important. Together we were going to set the equestrian world on fire."

Harry kissed her hot forehead. "Kate, you set *me* on fire. I don't know what is in our future, but I'd like to find out." He reached for both her hands and held them tightly. "Come to Boston. Pack up Jane, your parents, the horses, dogs, and even the attack chickens and come with me."

For a moment, temptation ran like wine in her veins. She searched his face and saw in his eyes an expression that looked like love.

Looking back at the rope swing, Kate dared herself to grab it and swing through the air. If the rope held, it would mean she should take a chance with Harry. If it broke, maybe she would fall, break her leg and get an extension on the court hearing.

"All of us?" She shook her head. "Sorry, Harry, but I can't see Guinea hens roosting in your closet."

She'd meant to lighten the moment, but Harry's eyes darkened. "What about if just you came? Even if it were just for a week or two."

He hadn't told her he loved her. Yet even if he had, would she believe him? When she was younger, she had always assumed that most relationships were like the one between her mother and father. Once the magical words, "I love you" were uttered, a radiant light beamed down, creating a bond between two people that couldn't be broken. When Roddy had told her that he loved her, she had thought she was stepping onto a path she knew well. Instead, it seemed the more she knew about love, the more it seemed to be a very slippery slope.

Kate's throat tightened. Was she willing to risk getting hurt again? It amazed her to realize how seriously she considered his offer. It was those eyes, looking down at her so quietly serious, so full of emotion.

"Harry, I appreciate the offer, but have you thought about how your family would react?" She gave a rueful smile. "Your brother made it pretty clear that he didn't want me to have contact with *anybody* in your family."

"Let me handle my family," Harry stated, but Kate wondered if he hadn't said it a bit too emphatically.

"I don't want to come between you and them." Kate crossed her arms on her chest. "You wouldn't be here if you didn't care deeply for them." She watched the creases on his forehead deepen. "I know firsthand how much Roddy and your mother depend on you."

"That doesn't mean that they get to choose what I do with my life."

"I'm not saying that, Harry, but like it or not, it's going to be a problem."

"That's what good lawyers are for, Kate, solving problems." He smiled smoothly, *a little too smoothly*, she thought. "First, I'm going to get you through the lawsuit on Monday, and then I'm going to convince you we can handle the personal stuff too."

"You are?" Kate wanted to believe him, but knew only too well that family ties were strong, especially when it came to looking after the people you loved. A man like Harry wouldn't take his obligations lightly and neither could she.

Chapter Sixteen

On Sunday evening, Harry looked out of the family room window at the steady stream of rain flowing down the glass. Every now and then the wind blew the rain harder, and it slashed against the window as if someone had thrown a handful of pebbles. Kate's words continued to fuel the conflict within him. *What do I really want to happen with Kate?*

"Harry?" The sharp edge to Jeb Withers' voice interrupted his thoughts. "How can you possibly think we can win this case considering we've got three new charges?" He ticked them off with his finger. "We've got a battery charge, a charge of voyeurism, and one count of vandalism."

Blinking, Harry tried to refocus his thoughts. He was supposed to be leading this emergency meeting. Tomorrow they faced Simon in court and Jeb had a point. Yet, ever since he and Kate had spoken of a future together, he'd been unable to think of anything else. He laced his fingers behind his head. Kate had been correct. If he pursued a relationship with her, it would come between him and Roddy. Was he willing to sacrifice this for a woman he barely knew?

Yet there was something deep inside him that insisted Kate belonged with him in Boston. First, he'd get her there, and then he'd show her the elementary school he'd attended, the softball field where he'd hit his first home run, and the stream behind his house where he'd spent hours reading beneath a birch tree. He'd take her to Cappy's grave. She would understand, more than anyone in the world, how much that labrador retriever had been part of his childhood.

And if all went as he believed, Kate would want to stay in Boston. He'd help her family relocate, too, if that was what they wanted. One of the things he admired most about Kate was the way she loved her family. He would not ask her to choose between them.

"Harry?" Jeb repeated. "Ignoring those charges won't make them go away."

"Everything will come together," he promised. *And if it doesn't*, he thought, *it'll be all the more reason for everyone to relocate to Boston.* "Let's have the committee reports."

"I'll start," Maureen volunteered. She pulled out a thick file of photographs. "I tailed Simon for twenty-four hours." She held up an eight-by-ten photograph of Simon in golfing briefs. "Told you the way he looks in underpants should be a crime." She flipped to the next photo. "Here's Simon at the First National Trust Company. Using my authority, I was able to uncover that he's in the process of applying for a loan."

Still trying to remove the sight of Simon in his underwear from his mind, Harry removed his glasses and rubbed his tired eyes. "Is his business in trouble?"

"No," Maureen said. "Don't you see? He's already

figured that if he wins, Kate's business will be closed permanently. He's preparing to make a play for her land."

"That's why we need to bury the assets," Jeb thundered.

"We'll win this," Harlan assured the old gentleman. "You have to think positively."

"Ask the captain of the *Titanic* if positive thinking would have kept his boat afloat." When no one answered, Jeb snorted in satisfaction.

"Point taken." Harry jotted some notes on his pad. "Any thing else, Maureen?"

"He pledged ten bucks to the highway patrol policemen's benevolence fund and then stiffed them." She shrugged at the neutral expression on Harry's face. "Shows his true character."

Shaking his head, Harry hid the smile threatening to break free. "Move along," he said. "Jimmy?"

"Twenty-five windshields broken within the past twelve months." Jimmy pushed a stack of invoices toward Harry. "I have documentation. Every one of those windshields was smashed by a golf ball."

"Excellent." Harry added Jimmy's documents to his file. "Harlan?"

Warming to his subject, Harlan shifted in the chair. "As you know, I've kept extensive records dating back to the nineteen-sixties. There's documentation on every rider that's ever passed through our gate." He cleared his throat. "In January nineteen-sixty . . ."

"Just give him the final numbers." Prissy softened her words with an affectionate squeeze of his hand. "Your written report has all the details he'll need."

Shrugging, Harlan pushed a thick pile of paper toward Harry. "In thirty years we've never gotten sued.

For a riding academy, that's practically unheard of."

"I've got references from leading horsemen and professionals." Prissy added her papers to the growing pile. "More double chocolate chip brownies, Harry?"

Why not? Harry winked at Kate.

Jane cleared her throat. "I'm ready with my report." Her eyes sparkled in anticipation.

As Jane rhapsodized about the benevolent animals, Harry found his attention wandering. He stole a glance at Kate, wishing she would meet his gaze. If he closed his eyes, he could almost smell the lemony fragrance of her shampoo, and feel the silk of her hair against his cheek. Although his invitation for Kate to come to Boston had been spontaneous, the more he thought about it, the greater it appealed. He'd never felt this way about any other woman. Could he be falling in love with her?

The idea seemed absurd. They hadn't spent enough time together to know each other well enough to call it love. Yet he couldn't deny how good he felt just to be around her. This feeling, he believed, would only grow stronger between them. Once the stable's legal affairs were put to rest, Harry felt certain he could convince Kate and her family to come to Boston with him. Of course, his mother would be horrified, but this was only to be expected from a woman who kept the Boston Social Registry by her bedside table. He could handle this, right?

"And then there was the time Houdini protected the Guinea hen babies when the chicken hawk attacked." Something about the pride in Jane's voice interrupted Harry's thoughts. "The Guinea hens scattered just as the hawk caught the mother. It would have flown off with her, but Houdini galloped over and scared it away.

"I remember that." Harlan stroked his chin. "We thought that bird would bleed to death."

"But all the other Guinea hens took care of it," Prissy added. "The male never left her side." She sighed. "Those birds have such a sense of *family*."

Family. The way Prissy said it made the small hairs on the back of Harry's neck stand straight.

"And there was the time a girl got hit on her shoulder with a golf ball," Jane continued. "It snapped her backward off the saddle. Houdini just stopped until she got her balance back. Another horse might have bucked that kid off. I wrote her testimony down too."

Harry's unease grew stronger. Somewhere in the middle of Jane's account of when Georgie scared off a trespassing golf player, the questions formed hard and fast. *Could Kate and her family be transplanted?*

All he had to do was look around the room and see eyes shining with love of the animals, of the life they'd built here. *They belonged.* Maybe he'd been too quick to think a fresh start would solve everyone's problems.

If Kate came to Boston, she had to leave her parents behind. Yet if she didn't, he'd have to give up his father's firm, or lose her. The rain on the window seemed ominous, a cold dose of reality. Either decision would require a sacrifice. Which did he want most?

Chapter Seventeen

"Good morning, your honor, I'm Melvin Albertson, representing Simon Trebeck, the owner of Crown Oaks golf course." The tall, dark-haired man stepped from behind the wooden desk and walked toward the judge. "I'm here today to shut down a business endangering the general public."

Albertson's sharp chin jutted forward, in a Jay Leno sort of way, but Kate saw neither humor nor warmth in the man's small eyes. He appeared mean, smart, and accustomed to winning.

In contrast, Jeb looked kindly but old, and to Kate's way of thinking, in the process of disappearing into his seat.

Albertson waved elegant, tapered fingers in Kate's direction. "Farm animals roam, an enormous dog stalks innocent golfers, wild birds attack people." He paused dramatically. "Horses stampede across a golf course." Albertson waved a piece of paper at the judge. "Just last week one of their horses knocked a woman unconscious."

Lifting his hands in a gesture that suggested these acts were too appalling for words, Albertson continued, "These people are negligent. They know it and they simply don't care. We intend to prove a willful disregard of the law in every area of their lives. We need to make their injunction permanent before someone is *killed*."

Albertson gave Kate a sad shake of his head. "*Killed*," he repeated in a tone that suggested she should hang her head in shame. Kate sat straighter in her seat. Just wait until the judge heard *their* opening speech.

She turned to her uncle with expectation. All heads in the silent courtroom turned to him as well. The elderly lawyer remained seated.

Okay, Kate thought, *Uncle Jeb is just sitting there doing nothing on purpose. I'm sure it's a legal tactic. Maybe he's building dramatic tension.* However, as Jeb remained seated, Kate had to reconsider. *Maybe it's stagefright.* She elbowed Harry who nudged Jeb, who leaped to his feet with the startled, slightly panicked look of a rabbit flushed from its hole.

"Good morning, your honor." His voice shook as noticeably as the hands holding the script Harry had prepared.

Wearing a tan, linen-blend suit, complete with a Fedora hat, Uncle Jeb resembled a nervous Colonel Sanders. His thick white mustache quivered. Kate was in agony that Jeb would faint on the floor.

"Your honor, I may look like that guy who invented Kentucky Fried Chicken, but my name is Jeb Withers. Yes, that's right, Withers, just like my client's. In fact, Harlan here, is my brother. This gives me a unique perspective. I know them better than any other lawyer in the world would—and as an officer of the court, I can completely vouch for their innocence," he paused, "and their animals' too." He smiled at the judge who did not return the look. "Our farm has been in business for half a century. Think about that, half a century, and nobody has ever questioned our integrity.

"We believe the charges against us are based on malice. Who gains if our riding academy is shut down permanently?" Jeb looked straight at Simon and pointed. "He does, your honor. He wants a shot at buying us out cheaply, and this is how he's gone about doing it."

Kate felt like cheering until she noticed the look of barely disguised disbelief on the judge's face. Only too well she remembered the other lawyers who had laughed outright when she'd sought their help.

She couldn't resist nodding in approval as Jeb returned to his seat. "Good job," she whispered.

The judge ordered, "Mr. Albertson, call your first witness."

"Simon Trebeck."

The golf course owner shot Kate a look of immense pleasure and righteous indignation as he took the stand.

"Mr. Trebeck," Albertson said, "How long have you been the owner of Crown Oaks Golf Course?"

"About two years."

"Tell us what it's been like running a private golf course across from the Withers' riding academy."

Simon produced a long-suffering sigh. "At first it was great. The Withers welcomed me warmly. They even gave me as much free fertilizer as I wanted."

"When did things start to change?"

"Almost immediately, although I didn't want to complain, so I put up with a lot."

"Like what?"

"Well, their chickens, for one." Simon smiled without humor at the judge. "They're over-sized and aggressive. Several golfers have had to seek medical attention after being pecked by these vicious birds."

"Objection," Jeb said. "They're not chickens. They're Guinea hens and it remains to be proved that these attacks actually happened."

"I may not call them by the right name," Simon replied, "but I know when I'm being pecked." A ripple of laughter spread through the courtroom.

"Overruled." The judge banged her gavel.

"And then their dog began attacking my golfers." Simon looked up at the judge. "The dog weighs more than one hundred pounds, your honor. At times it strays onto our course. Judge, golfers have driven their carts into the water hazard in self-defense."

"Following the outbreak of these attacks, did you, or did you not, ask the Withers to fortify and raise the height of their fence?"

"I did. I even sent them a copy of the New York State code, stating all fences containing animals should be secure enough to keep animals out of the road." He paused, sniffed, and added, "The minimum recommended height is forty-eight inches."

"Did the Withers family do anything?"

"Nothing." Simon sniffed more loudly. "It's been a miracle no one has been *killed*."

Kate stiffened in her seat. "Wish Georgie had bitten Simon in the jugular."

"Don't worry." Harry patted her hand. "Jeb'll do that for us."

"And the escaped pony?" Albertson prompted.

Simon nodded. "Just last week, the Withers family

let its pony romp across my golf course. One of my golfers hit a tree in his cart while trying to escape its path. Other club members were nearly trampled when the beast galloped wildly through the concession area. My facilities received extensive damage."

"Objection," Jeb shouted. "Kate didn't let the pony loose on purpose."

"Oh, they unleashed the beast on purpose," Simon said in a growl from the witness box. "They sent it like an attack dog to hunt me down and as many of my members as possible."

"Objection," Jeb declared. "These are unsubstantiated, outrageous statements. The witness cannot possibly know my client's intent."

The judge banged her gavel. "Sustained."

Albertson paced in front of the witness box. "Can you tell us, Mr. Trebeck, the extent of the damage the pony caused?"

"Absolutely." Simon held up a photographic enlargement showing overturned tables, golfers sprawled on the ground, shattered dishes and food everywhere. "This photo was taken shortly after the pony charged through my golf course, trampling everything in his way."

Albertson handed the photo to the judge, who stared at it and frowned.

"Why do you think Miss Withers purposely released the pony?" Albertson asked.

"Because hoofprints on my green are the surest way to destroy my business. She wants me to reroute the golf course so that my golfers don't come so close to her precious horses."

Albertson glanced up at the judge to make sure she'd gotten this point. He all but waited for her to write on her legal pad before he asked the next question.

"Why close the whole stable down permanently?" Albertson stood very close to his client and looked at him as sympathetically as his wolf-like eyes would allow. "Why not simply get rid of the pony?"

Simon shook his head. "They have no control over their business." He paused. "A few nights ago these people vandalized my fence. Not to mention spied on me." He pointed at Kate. "Those people are an accident waiting to happen."

"No further questions." Albertson's eyes blazed with triumph. He strutted back to his seat. "Your witness."

Rising, Jeb slowly crossed the room to the witness stand. He cleared his throat several times in the silent room. "Isn't it true your golfers find it amusing to aim at cars parked in the Withers' lot?"

"Of course not." Simon shrugged. "I'm not saying we've never hit a golf ball onto their property. However, it's never been deliberate."

"Then how do you explain twenty-five broken windshields over the past sixteen months?" Jeb produced a stack of invoices with such a flourish that Harry pumped his fist.

Simon exclaimed. "It's an exaggeration!"

Jeb handed the report to the judge. "We have documentation."

"He's trying to change the focus of this hearing," Simon sputtered. "What's important is to realize the Withers can't control their animals."

"That's not true," Prissy shouted. "You're the one who has no control. Your golfers couldn't find the eighth hole with a seeing-eye dog."

"Mrs. Withers, you will get your turn," the judge called sternly. She turned to Simon. "You do seem to have broken a lot of windshields."

Simon flushed. "Mishits. They're mishits. Our fairway lines up with her parking lot, judge."

"And don't your golfers often try and retrieve their golf balls after they've hit them onto the Withers' property?" Jeb continued.

"Upon occasion."

"Aren't they afraid of the so-called vicious animals?"

Kate grinned. *Go Uncle Jeb*, she thought. She shot Harry a sideways look. He squeezed her hand in encouragement.

"We caution the golfers, but they don't always take our warning seriously." Simon paused. "Until it's too late."

Jeb frowned, obviously not wanting to end on this note. "Isn't it true Mr. Trebeck, that should the Withers' farm be offered for sale, you would be willing to purchase it?"

"I'd consider it, I'm a business man."

"Of course you are, but what we don't know is how far you're willing to go in order to make sure that land comes up for sale."

"Objection," Albertson roared.

"Withdrawn," Jeb said. "No further questions."

Sinking onto the straight-backed wooden chair, Jeb mopped his face with his handkerchief and closed his eyes.

Kate patted his shoulder. "Great job."

"Your honor," Albertson said, standing. "I could put a lot of witnesses up here to testify about animals straying onto the golf course, but in the interests of time, I'd like to go right to the source of all this trouble." He paused. "We call Katherine Withers."

Chapter Eighteen

Harry's fists clenched as Kate made her way to the witness stand. Lawyers like Albertson would twist Kate's words, distort the facts, and rattle her with every legal trick in the book. His heart ached to see her up there alone.

He locked his gaze with Jeb's and hoped he understood his fears and was prepared to jump to Kate's defense.

Albertson ran his fingers through his dark hair. "The height of your fence isn't up to code, is it?"

"We're working on it."

"Just answer yes or no."

"No," Kate replied. "Not entirely."

"In fact, the fence does little or nothing." Albertson looked up at the judge as if he was making sure he had her attention before he asked the next question. "Your dog attacks golfers, doesn't she?"

Kate frowned. "No."

Albertson lowered his voice. "Oh, come on Miss

Withers, we have affidavits from respected members of the community who say otherwise."

Shrugging, Kate focused her gaze on Harry, who gave his most reassuring nod. "She retrieves the golf balls they hit onto our property."

"Retrieves them?" Albertson sneered. "I'd say she mauls them." He pointed to a stack of affidavits. "One golfer drove his cart into a tree while fleeing your dog. Another had to be towed out of the water hazard."

"They're liars." Prissy shouted. "Not to mention incredibly lousy drivers."

"Mrs. Withers," the judge said as she banged her gavel. "I'm going to have to ask you to leave if you can't be quiet."

"Georgie has never hurt anyone," Kate cried.

"If the dog isn't enough, then there's the wild birds." Albertson leaned over the witness box. "One man had to seek medical attention, didn't he?"

"He tore his pants diving through our fence," Kate stated.

"Because he feared for his life, didn't he?"

Jeb stood up. "Objection, your honor, Miss Withers cannot possibly know what someone else thought."

"I'll allow it for now."

"He might have been afraid," Kate admitted.

"Isn't it true that the bulk of the stable's operations rest on your shoulders?"

Kate glanced at her parents. "My mother does the books and my father teaches lessons as well. Everyone helps with the stable chores."

Albertson held up Kate's appointment book. "According to your records, prior to the stable's closing, you taught forty lessons a week. Your father taught five. I'd say you're doing the majority of the work."

Kate didn't respond. Harry sensed the direction of Albertson's questions. He had the sick feeling Albertson was about to go for blood and there wasn't a darn thing he could do.

"Isn't it a bit too much?" Albertson asked sympathetically. "Teaching all those lessons, keeping track of your boarders, looking after your daughter?"

"No, it isn't too much."

"Oh, I think it is. Your parents are getting older and more and more responsibility has been dumped on you." Albertson leaned over the witness box at Kate. "You can't handle it. You can't control your animals. Admit it. The stable is out of control."

"No it's not," Kate said fiercely.

"Call an objection." Harry nudged Jeb.

"Objection."

"Over-ruled," the judge replied. "Both times."

"Didn't one of your horses recently knock a woman unconscious?"

"Yes, but—"

"Another horse annihilated Mr. Trebeck's fence?"

"Objection," Harry called, rising to his feet. "Counsel is using inflammatory language. Breaking a post is hardly annihilating a fence."

"Over-ruled."

"You haven't had a vacation in years," Albertson continued. "Why is that? Are you afraid of leaving your parents alone with the stable?"

"Of course not." Kate flushed, forming to Harry's eyes an unmistakable look of guilt. He pressed his pen so tightly on the pad the point made a hole in the paper.

"Hasn't your daughter recently been sent to the

principal's office for wearing inappropriate clothing?"
Albertson leaned over Kate. "You can't even control
what your daughter wears, can you?"

"Objection," Harry shouted, completely forgetting
he wasn't the lawyer in charge.

"Quiet," the judge shouted, pointing at Harry. "Or
you will be removed from the court." She turned to
Kate. "The witness will answer the question."

"Of course I can control my daughter," Kate said.
"As much as any parent can control her child."

Harry elbowed Jeb. He didn't like Albertson accusing Kate of poor parenthood. "This line of questioning
is completely irrelevant," he whispered.

"I know it," Jeb replied, "but there's nothing we can
do about it."

"Was it an accident when you let an untrained pony
destroy a golf course and endanger golfers?" Albertson
continued.

"Yes," Kate shot back. "I mean I didn't let him
loose on purpose. It was an accident." She looked at
the judge. "You can't keep animals tied up all the
time. Things like this happen at every barn."

Harry's jaw tightened. He smelled blood, unfortu-
nately, Kate's blood. He sensed Albertson building to
a finish.

"So you're saying it's likely one of your animals
will escape again."

"No." Kate looked at Harry who could only hold
her gaze. "I mean, we're like any other stable."

"I wonder how many other accidents we don't know
about," Albertson said. "Could it be that you're simply
overwhelmed by the responsibility of running a stable
by yourself? I understand that you don't even have a
college degree." Albertson's voice rose to a shout.
"Isn't it true you're in over your head?"

"Objection," Harry shouted, jumping up. He leaned as far over the desk as gravity would allow. "Objection, counsel is badgering the witness."

"Enough," the judge ordered. "This is your last warning. Do you hear me?"

Harry nodded. "Yes, your honor."

"Mr. Albertson," the judge said, "please continue."

"Your business isn't a respected riding academy," Albertson said. "It's the local joke, a falling down barn with untrained horses and inept management."

"Objection," Jeb called. "Where's the question?"

Albertson smiled meanly. "Right here. How long were you married, Miss Withers?"

"Objection," Jeb shouted. "Irrelevant."

"Your honor, if you'll allow me to continue, you'll see this information is crucial to my client's case."

The judge leaned down. "Witness will answer the question."

"A little over a year," Kate replied. She looked at Harry, who knew his eyes mirrored the same worry.

"It was fifteen months to be exact," Albertson replied. "I looked it up when we took this case." He paused. "It was no surprise to see Mr. Jeb Withers' name on the divorce documents, but imagine my shock to discover the name of the presiding judge was James Kirk. While he made a great captain of the starship Enterprise, as a licensed judge, he doesn't exist." He let the information sink in. "In short, fraud was committed." He pointed to Jeb, who stood seemingly struck dumb. "In conclusion, these people," and he gestured toward Jeb, Harry, and Kate, "have no respect for the law whatsoever."

"Objection," Harry shouted, the chair toppling behind him. "This is way over the line."

"Counsel, approach the bench," the judge ordered.

Harry barreled to the front of the room, beating Jeb and Albertson by a good two steps. He couldn't believe no one had seen this coming. A small voice at the back of his head calmly pointed out that he would have expected this if he hadn't been so busy imagining the life he might have with Kate in Boston.

"I asked the counselors to approach," the judge said, glaring down at him. "Not *you.*"

Harry felt her dislike pouring over him like a cold shower. He squared his shoulders. "Your honor, I am a lawyer." He kept his tone polite and professional. "Practicing out of Boston, Massachusetts." He ignored the look of intense disbelief she gave him. "And it appears to me that even if the matter Mr. Albertson has just brought to your attention was relevant, it's already been corrected."

"You don't think this judge needs to know that Mr. Withers committed fraud against the court?" Albertson paused. "He's probably involved in the coverup. Maybe we should add his name when we notify the bar association."

"Go right ahead," Harry challenged, "and see what happens." He leaned into the other man, boiling for a fight in a way he never had before.

"Gentlemen!" The judge pounded her gavel. She looked at Jeb. "Is it true? Did you forge a judge's signature on Miss Withers' divorce papers?"

In the sudden silence, Jeb's face turned a brilliant shade of red. "I didn't forge the signature, but I did make a mistake."

"One that he covered up for nearly a decade," Albertson pointed out. "Don't you wonder what else they're hiding? The entire family is dishonest." He jerked his thumb at Harry. "Him too."

"Enough," the judge hissed. She looked at each lawyer closely. "I don't know who's telling the truth here, but I do know that some disturbing charges have been made. In all good conscience, I'm going to have to ask Mr. Withers to excuse himself from the defense until this other matter gets cleared up. I'll give the Withers one week to find themselves another lawyer. Until then the temporary injunction against their business stands."

She lifted her gavel, but Harry's voice stopped her mid-swing. "Your honor," he said, "if it's agreeable to the court, I can represent the Withers." He smiled wryly, "I'm well familiar with the case."

She gave him another look that suggested this was about as good an idea as lying down in a bed of poison ivy. "You aren't even licensed in New York."

"By reason of pro ad hoc," Harry replied, "you could allow this." He could have tried another one of his best smiles but instead opted for something he knew would have greater appeal. "That way we could settle this matter today. You wouldn't have to go through all the testimony again."

The judge lifted an eyebrow in speculation. After a moment, she turned to Albertson. "I'm inclined to grant his request. Any objections?"

"The Withers can put their Guinea hens in charge of their defense for all I care," Albertson snorted. "The facts of this case are going to speak for themselves. Not even Johnny Cochran could save them."

"The court is in recess until one this afternoon," the judge ordered. "When we return, Mr. Bond will be representing the Withers." She stared Harry straight in the eye. "All parties will be on their best behavior or they will be held in contempt of court." She banged the gavel. "Adjourned."

"Well," said Kate, as they walked outside the court-house, "I don't think that went so well."

That's the understatement of the century, Harry thought. *It's going to take a miracle to win this case.*

"It's not over yet." Prissy jerked open her over-sized purse and pulled out a plastic zip-lock bag full of cookies.

What's she going to do, Harry wondered, *bribe the judge with oatmeal raisin bars?* He didn't dare voice his fears, just in case she hadn't thought of it yet.

"Here, dear." Prissy handed her husband the first bar. "Have a sweet. We all should. It'll help keep our spirits up."

Harlan took the cookie. "The judge just can't ignore our safety record."

Kate leaned back against the hood of the Buick and surveyed the rest of the cars in the lot. "I blew it, didn't I? Albertson got me rattled."

"You didn't do that bad," Maureen said, joining them. "Until they brought up your divorce." She shook her head in disbelief. "How in the world do you suppose Albertson found out?"

"Maybe someone overheard me and Harry on the golf course." Kate turned to Harry. "Remember? That first day you came? We weren't exactly alone when you told me about Roddy wanting to remarry. One of Simon's cronies must have told Simon, who told Albertson."

Jeb rubbed his face. "It's all my fault, Kate. I'm so sorry about messing up your divorce." His face wrinkled in regret. "I just wanted everything done quickly so you could put this behind you."

Kate squeezed his arm. "It's okay." She tilted her chin to look up at him. "I'm sorry too. None of this would have come out if you weren't representing us today." She tried to smile but her lips trembled. "You won't get disbarred, will you?"

"Disbarred?" Prissy pushed another cookie into Jeb's hand. "That isn't going to happen, is it?"

"Maybe if I retire," Jeb said and bit into the raisin bar, "I can avoid being disbarred."

"This is all Simon's fault," Maureen said. "That greedy fool. God help him if he ever double parks in my beat."

"We're not done yet." *Although it looks pretty bad,* Harry thought, but didn't voice. He didn't have the heart to remind Kate that Jeb's future wasn't the only thing at stake. If the injunction against her business became permanent, Simon might seek financial reparation as the next step.

Harry looked at his clenched fists and slowly let his fingers open. Despite the cool autumn day, his face felt flushed and hot. He wondered how many hundreds of times he had been in court and gotten angry. Never had he been on the verge of punching someone in the nose. Then again, he'd never gotten so involved with a client before.

Albertson was only doing his job, which was to discredit Kate. But when he'd attacked Kate personally, Harry had been ready to rip the man's throat out. He'd never come close to attacking another lawyer physically. Not only that, never had he felt this vague sensation of regret that he hadn't.

Harry stroked his chin thoughtfully. "We need something drastic."

"Like what?" Kate asked.

Harry had no idea. At this point, Albertson would probably be able to discredit any character witness that he put on the stand. No. He needed something that couldn't be challenged—something that would remove any doubt in the judge's mind that the Withers had wild, untrained animals.

If he could convince the judge that the animals were safe, maybe he could get her to give them some leeway about the fence height. Wait a minute. What if he could prove the animals were safe?

"I have an idea." Harry gave them the details.

Chapter Nineteen

At one o'clock sharp, Harry addressed the judge.

"Mr. Albertson suggests that the Withers cannot be trusted to tell the truth. Their character, their business acumen, even their honor has been called into question."

Sweat prickled Harry's back. "The facts do seem to favor Mr. Albertson's position. However, there are extenuating circumstances that prove, beyond reasonable doubt, that my client is a victim of a malicious campaign designed to put her out of business."

He sounded ridiculous. Even if he hadn't seen the skepticism in the judge's eyes he would have realized this. If anyone from his firm had been there, they would have laughed themselves silly. They would have told him he was making a fool of himself by taking on a case involving fence heights and pecking chickens. They would have accused him of an inappropriate and unprofessional relationship with a client. They would be right.

Harry took a deep breath. "We call Harlan Withers to the stand."

In the witness box, Harlan settled himself into the seat with the air of a man prepared to be there quite a while.

"Tell the court about your stable's history," Harry said, "with attention to its safety record and policies."

Crossing his arms, Harry spread his stance. Hopefully he'd be standing there for quite a while. For his plan to work, Kate needed time.

Harlan stroked his chin thoughtfully. "To do that," he said, "we must start at the beginning. In September nineteen-fifty-eight we began holding English riding lessons."

By the time Harlan reached the 1970s, half the room had cleared out. The other half hadn't moved in quite a while, and appeared to be sleeping in sitting positions. Harlan's deep voice droned on and on. Even Albertson, who initially had enthusiastically challenged Harlan, now sat slumped. He didn't even bother to challenge Harlan's figures, when a short time later, the old horseman summarized the stable's record.

"No questions," Albertson declared. "I'm just glad my fee is based on an hourly sum."

Someone in the courtroom laughed. Harry checked his watch. "We call Mrs. Priscilla Withers."

The bag of cookies bulged noticeably from the top of Prissy's bag. Harry wondered if she'd left the bag open on purpose. As the heavenly perfume of home-baked cookies wafted through the air, Harry almost reconsidered his earlier position on their effectiveness as a bribe.

"Mrs. Withers, can you tell us about these Guinea hens which seem to be terrorizing golfers?"

"Objection," Albertson cried. "Mrs. Withers is no authority on these birds. Besides, the Withers have had plenty of time to defend their case."

Harry shot to his feet. "Your honor, Mrs. Withers has raised these birds for more than twenty years. How can my client defend the charges against her stable if you don't allow her to answer the question?"

The judge looked at her watch, and then her gaze fixed on Prissy's bag of oatmeal raisin cookies. Harry saw the longing in her eyes. "I'd like to have a good raisin, I mean good reason, to rule in your favor, Mr. Albertson, but I don't." She sniffed. "Witness will answer the question."

Prissy nodded, and happily launched into a lengthy explanation of the Guinea hen psyche. "In conclusion, the only reason to be afraid," she stated, "is if you're a flea or a tick. Guinea hens eat them."

During the next half hour, Harry showed enlargements of the area of fence that he and Kate had modified with wood from the dismantled shed. He spoke of the financial necessity of reopening the stable in order to raise the rest of the fence. However, as Harry studied the thin line of the judge's lips, he knew she'd reached a decision he wouldn't like. He hoped Kate had had enough time to implement his plan. "We have one final witness."

The judge sighed. "Mr. Bond, I'm ready to make my ruling. I've got six other cases pending today."

Harry smiled. "This last witness won't take very long, your honor."

"I've heard enough, Mr. Bond." She raised her gavel. "In the motion to make permanent the injunction against the Withers' Riding Academy—"

"Your honor," Harry interrupted. "You wouldn't be thinking of violating my client's rights, would you?"

The judge hesitated, "Proceed, Mr. Bond, but make it snappy!"

Harry smiled. "We call Houdini."

Chapter Twenty

Albertson exploded from his seat. "Your honor!"

His voice, Harry noted, had gone hoarse, and the words came out sounding like, "Your horror."

"You do realize he's called a horse into your courtroom?"

"With all due respect, your honor," Harry replied, "it's not only the Withers on trial, but also their animals. Mr. Trebeck claims they endanger the general public. You need to see first hand the wildest of them all—the Shetland pony that tore up the golf course."

"It isn't just the pony!" Albertson shouted. "It's the dog and the rest of the animals on that funny farm."

"We're prepared to bring those to court as well," Harry said calmly. "First, we thought we'd start with the pony."

"A pony in my court?" The judge studied Harry's face. "You're kidding, right?"

"It's the heart of our defense," Harry improvised. "The pony poses no danger to anybody. You need to see it for yourself."

"We've already seen the damage this pony has caused," Albertson insisted loudly. "He's a four-legged tornado."

"I'm going to allow this." The judge shook her head. "Although you may regret this, Mr. Bond."

Harry raised his voice. "Okay, Kate." It amazed him in the seconds that followed, to find himself enjoying the case in a way he never would have believed.

The back doors to the courtroom swung open. The head and neck of a plump brown pony peeked inside. Someone sighed, a sound gathering volume as others joined in.

Houdini looked at everyone through long, brown bangs that all but covered his eyes. Following Kate, he stepped forward, his unshod hooves pinging on the polished, hardwood floors.

Three little girls sat bareback on the pony's broad, hairy back. They grinned and waved as Houdini carried them solemnly through the courtroom. The Shetland held his head high, as if aware his behavior spoke for his entire species.

Harry waited until the pony halted at the front of the room. "Your honor," he said, "this is Houdini."

At Kate's signal, Houdini offered his front leg in a handshake. The courtroom applauded enthusiastically, with the exception of the group sitting behind Simon.

The judge got up from her seat. She studied Houdini from every angle. "He appears to be a very calm pony."

"He's probably drugged," cried Albertson.

"We are willing to submit the pony to drug testing," Harry declared.

"And who are his little jockeys?" The judge smiled at the three beaming faces.

"These are some of Houdini's regular riders," Harry replied.

Albertson shot up, waving his hands in an obvious attempt to frighten the pony. "We object. This is a blatant attempt to manipulate the judge's decision."

The pony stuck out its lower lip at the red-faced attorney as the audience howled with laughter.

For the first time the judge frowned at the tall, dark-haired lawyer. "I'll determine if their testimony is coached. I may not know much about horses, but I know quite a bit about liars."

The judge turned to the first little girl sitting on Houdini. "How old are you dear?"

"Five," the little girl replied.

"Ever fall off Houdini?"

"No way. He stops if you lose your balance." The girl's long eyelashes swept her cheeks. "When I ride him, he has to stop lots of times."

"How about you?" The judge motioned to the next rider. "What's your name?"

The girl made a noise that was not quite comprehensible. "Nora is deaf. She signs." A small woman stepped forward. "I'm her mother, Debbie Struthers, and I'll be glad to translate."

"By all means." The judge sighed. "Ask if Houdini is gentle."

Mrs. Struthers translated the judge's words.

"She says that Houdini is a very gentle pony, and that riding him is her favorite thing in the world."

"Your honor," Albertson sputtered. "The testimony of three little girls hardly proves anything."

"You had your turn." The judge turned to the third girl. "I suppose you adore Houdini as well."

"Yes," the little girl said.

"And you've never fallen off him?"

"Well," the little girl said, "I almost fell off when I got hit by a golf ball. Luckily Houdini stopped in time."

"Objection," Albertson shouted. "The witness has been coached."

Harry shrugged. "She's telling the truth."

"What did you do, offer a year's worth of free riding lessons?" Albertson put his hands on the desk and glared in anger at the little girl.

The pony whinnied, and Albertson jumped back so fast his chair nearly toppled over.

"Are you sure?" the judge asked.

"Yes. Miss Kate let me keep the ball." She reached in her pocket. "Here it is."

"This is outrageous," Albertson cried. "The word of a five-year-old girl."

"This changes things," the judge said thoughtfully.

"This changes nothing." Albertson's olive complexion darkened. His breath became ragged. "Surely you can't let the word of three five-year-old girls sway your decision."

"If you don't want to take the word of three five-year-olds," Harry said, "you can ask any of these riders about the safety of Kate's horses."

The back door to the courtroom opened again, and an army of girls wearing riding boots and hard hats marched into the room. Leading the way was Georgie, whose tail wagged at high speed.

"Every one of these riders will testify to the safety of my client's riding academy." Harry allowed himself to look at Kate, who grinned back at him. He couldn't ever remember seeing a more beautiful smile on a woman's face.

"Oh good heavens." The judge shook her head at the group of girls, circling the pony protectively.

Harry raised his voice over the excited chatter from the spectators. "My client admits that Houdini got loose on the course, and is willing to pay reasonable damages."

Georgie, by this time, had reached the judge and dropped a golf ball at her feet as if it were an offering. The judge smiled and began to stroke the dog's face.

"Your honor," Albertson cried, "the very fact that the Withers would bring so many people and animals into your courtroom is evidence of their lack of concern for the safety of the public."

"We care very much!" Kate yelled back. "If the judge doubts this, she's invited to come to the stable and take a riding lesson herself."

"Not if my life depended on it," the judge replied as she retreated to the safety of her bench. Georgie followed, as if the judge were her long, lost friend. When the judge sat, Georgie sat next to her with her head tilted at the exact same angle.

The judge put her hand on Georgie's head. "I had a dog like you growing up. Her name was Inky."

Georgie grinned, revealing long rows of glistening white teeth.

"These animals are no danger to anybody," the judge proclaimed. "Based on this, and the good-faith attempt to raise the fence to the required height, I'm lifting the temporary injunction against Miss Withers' stable. Furthermore, I'm ordering both parties to enter into a letter of agreement whereby Miss Withers will have six months to raise the capital she needs to bring the fence up to code as outlined by New York statute."

The judge paused. "I'm giving you a second chance,

Miss Withers, but be aware that I never want to see you," she paused and looked hard at Harry, "or you, in my court ever again. Now, get these animals out of my courtroom!" She banged her gavel. "Court adjourned!"

Chapter Twenty-One

With Houdini safely loaded in the horse trailer, and Georgie lying at her feet, Kate sank back against the hub of the trailer. She crossed her arms and struggled to let everything sink in. Harry had done it. They hadn't lost the stable after all.

She should have felt like celebrating. Instead, it seemed a miracle that her heart managed to beat at all. With the charges dismissed, nothing further prevented her from giving Harry an answer.

Her mother caught her eye and winked across the parking lot. She and her father wore matching triumphant grins. Little girls danced through the parking lot, shouting in excitement and chanting Houdini's name.

Kate's gaze traveled past the scene to the courtroom doors. Harry remained inside, finalizing the paperwork. Did she care enough to go with him to Boston? It seemed an impossible question. Certainly, he had touched her life in a way she could never have anticipated. Yet he had not spoken of love, and although she told herself this would come in time, it still bothered her.

The doors swung open and Harry stepped out of the courthouse. His gaze scanned the parking lot and softened when he saw her. In response, her heartbeat accelerated until the beats seemed to blur together. Harry hurried through the crowd toward her. He took her hands and squeezed them. "We did it, Kate. Congratulations."

"Because of you." Her hands gripped his tightly.

"*We* did it." Harry looked long and hard into her eyes. "The two of us."

Kate nodded, dreading the unavoidable question and determined to prolong it as long as possible. "You were brilliant to think of bringing the kids and the animals to our defense."

"It was Jane's idea, actually."

"Well, I couldn't believe that you made Houdini your star witness." Kate shook her head in wonder.

"It was a bit outside my normal strategy. However, I would have put my grandmother on the stand if it would have helped take down that slimy Albertson." He shook his head. "He never should have gone after you personally."

"He didn't look so arrogant at the end. In fact, he looked about ready to cry."

"He did, didn't he?" Harry grinned.

"I don't think he's ever lost a case due to the testimony of a Shetland pony."

"I think your parents are giving an interview to a reporter. Looks like you might even make the local news tonight. It'll be good for your business."

"What about Uncle Jeb? What's going to happen to him?"

Harry shrugged. "Hopefully nothing. It was an honest mistake. I'll be glad to get involved on his behalf." He smiled. "If it weren't for his mistake, I would never have met you."

Kate nodded. She braved another look into Harry's eyes and braced herself for the inevitable question.

Reaching for both her hands, Harry lifted them gently. "Will you come to Boston?"

Kate met his gaze. The answer had been clear for some time, but she hadn't wanted to admit it. "Will you stay in New York?"

Harry's eyes darkened and his grip tightened. "It wouldn't make sense. My career is in Boston." His mouth produced a smile that looked stiff and uncomfortable. "We could buy a new farm in Boston. Besides, Jane needs to get to know my side of the family as well as yours."

Kate swallowed the lump in her throat. Harry's side of the family had no interest in Jane. Even if there wasn't that to consider, she knew her parents would never agree to move. They needed her help. She couldn't just leave them.

"We'll even bring the Guinea hens." Harry tipped her chin to look into her eyes. "A fresh start, Kate, for all of us."

"I appreciate the offer, Harry. Truly. But it's too big a step, for me, for Jane, and for my parents." She tried to smile and failed. "Besides, you know I'd never be accepted by your family. You'd end up hating me."

Harry's brow wrinkled. "Come on, Kate. We've only known each other a short time, but it's the right thing." He paused. "We belong together."

"I can't go." Kate could barely whisper the words.

"I can't stay." Harry bent his head lower. She heard

the confusion in his voice. "My dad left me in charge of the firm. People are depending on me."

"I know it."

"I can't stay here."

"I know."

"You understand why I have to go, don't you?"

"Yes." Kate twisted her hands together. "The strange thing is that I really do." Her lips trembled.

Harry looked stricken, but determined. "Just come for a week then. Give us more time to figure things out."

"I can't do that." Kate gazed past his left shoulder, at the tops of the buildings and horizon beyond.

"Yes you can." Harry gripped her hand. "Just do it. For me, if you can't do it for yourself."

"We'd just have to go through the same thing a week from now, Harry."

Harry studied her eyes, said, "Oh heck," and kissed her.

Kate barely had time to register Harry's arms gripping her like a vise when his lips clamped down on her mouth. She grabbed his neck, melted into his body, and kissed him back with everything she had.

Maureen, who was busy checking Melvin Albertson's vehicle inspection sticker, glanced up as Jimmy tapped her shoulder. "Take a look at our Kate."

A huge smile stretched across Maureen's narrow face. "Go Katie," she said. "About time."

"When was the last time you saw two people so much in love?" Jimmy's large brown eyes looked at Maureen wistfully.

"Never. I hope someone here knows CPR because I don't think either one of them is coming up for air."

Jimmy fingered his thick mustache. "Harry's fixing the mixup in the paperwork for my divorce. As soon as it's final, will you marry me?"

"Marry you?" Maureen's cheeks flushed, and she grabbed Jimmy by the shoulders and kissed him. When she looked up, she said, "Yes, I'll marry you." She kissed him again. "I can't believe it."

Jimmy opened his eyes. "Believe it, baby. I'm good for much more than that."

"Oh no." Maureen pointed at Kate. "She's crying. I've never seen her do that, not even after the rat left her."

"Maybe she's just happy. Women do that."

"Look at her—that's not happiness." She pointed to a black SUV pulling out of the parking lot. "That's Harry's car." Maureen bit her lip thoughtfully. "I'll call in an APB on him. Get him pulled over or something. If he's in jail, he can't leave."

Jimmy shook his head. "Don't jump into anything Maureen."

Maureen didn't speak for a moment, but her eyes never left Kate. "I've got to talk to her."

She marched over to Kate. "If you want him, I'll go get him. Say the word."

Kate wiped her eyes. She shook her head. "He wants to go to Boston, Maureen. Let him."

Maureen put her arm around Kate's shoulders. "I can make him stay." She squeezed her friend. "My cousin works the Massachusetts Pike tollbooth. We can stop him there."

Kate shook her head. "He made his choice and it wasn't me." She reached for the tissue that Jimmy offered and blew hard.

"He chose wrong." Maureen patted Kate's shoulder. "He chose wrong."

"What am I going to do without him?" Kate looked at her friend through a blur of tears.

"You'll be fine," Maureen said. Her expression was gentle. "We'll give him a month to come to his senses. If he doesn't, you and me, we'll go up there and get him."

Jimmy moaned and looked unhappier than ever. "We'll all end up in jail."

"That's not a bad idea," Maureen said brightly. "If we're in jail, we could call Harry. He'd come defend you. I know he would."

"I'm not going to jail just to get Harry back," Kate said in a strangled voice. "It's over." She lifted her shoulders. "All in all," she said, trying to joke, "I'm sticking to horses from now on."

Maureen just smiled. "I'll look up the route to Boston, just in case."

Chapter Twenty-Two

The heat of the horses warmed the frosty air. A light snow had fallen the night before and it banked against the windows, and muffled the sound of the wind in the trees.

In the early morning darkness, Kate shivered in her thick down jacket and tried to ignore the cold tingling in her fingers as she dumped grain into buckets. As she worked, Georgie happily sniffed out a golf ball hidden in a pile of hay, then collapsed onto the concrete floor.

The rich scent of the horses and the hay filled Kate's nose. She smiled as a horse kicked out impatiently and another answered with a loud neigh. "I know, I know. Your breakfast is coming."

It had been six weeks since Harry had left. Six long weeks and he hadn't called once. She didn't blame him. What was the point? They'd both made their choice. She tried to convince herself that the dull throb she felt was because she'd recently hit her thumb with a hammer, but all this did was remind her of Harry's

172

warning about tools and make her feel worse than ever.

I don't need him, she reminded herself as she reached Houdini's stall. *I'm perfectly capable of being happy without a man.*

As she lifted the metal grain scoop, something overhead moved. Her gaze went to the ceiling where tiny drifts of hay floated down. *That's funny. It sounds like someone's walking around up there. It must be the Guinea hens.* Frowning, she returned to feeding the horses.

Goosebumps pebbled her back as the floor boards above her creaked. *Someone's up there.* Kate looked around for a weapon. In the semi-darkness, the idea of a stranger in her loft sent her heart thumping. She looked at the big, black dog. "Do you hear anything, Georgie?"

The dog grinned and wagged its tail.

"Okay, if you're so happy about this, you can go and check the loft."

Georgie licked Kate's cold fingers. "Oh, all right." Kate stroked the dog's sleek head. "You're more likely to lick someone than bite them anyway."

Her gaze fell on a pitchfork leaning against the wall. Tucking it beneath her arm, she walked over to the medal ladder. Pausing, she listened a final time. "Is there anyone up there?"

In the ensuing silence, Kate wondered if she'd made up the whole thing. However, she was determined to investigate. With a final glance at Georgie, who cocked her head as if she couldn't believe her owner would act so strangely, Kate climbed the ladder.

The pitchfork clanked on each rung and she nearly stabbed herself in the toe twice before reached the top.

Straining her eyes, she looked around the nearly pitch-black room. Her gaze immediately went to the over-sized window. *I didn't leave the door open, did I?* The thought had no sooner passed through her brain when a tall, solid-looking man stepped out of the shadows.

The pitchfork fell to the ground. Kate's shaking legs urged her to do the same. "Harry?" She squinted. *Am I dreaming?*

"Hello, Kate."

Looking strong and sexy in faded blue jeans, Harry smiled at her. She watched his lips form her name and the way his breath evaporated.

Lit by the earliest shades of the sunrise, Harry's face was even more handsome than she remembered. He'd cropped his hair short and it seemed dark against the sand color of his skin.

"Harry, what are you doing here?"

His smile was slow and crooked and warmed the room a notch. "Admiring the sunrise. You get a great view from here."

He looked so pleased with himself that Kate wanted to pick up the pitchfork and push him right out the open window. Why hadn't he called or written? "Aren't you supposed to be in Boston?" She heard the hurt and anger in her voice.

"Nope." The smile broadened on Harry's face. "You don't sound happy to see me."

"Why should I be happy to see you again?" Kate looked longingly at the pitchfork.

Harry pulled a letter out of his pocket. "Because I'm here to solve your legal problems. I've been hired again."

Kate wanted to snatch the letter from his hands. She could easily guess that Maureen had written Harry with some trumped up legal problem just to get him to come back. Knowing Maureen, it could be anything from murder to chronic shop lifting.

"Whatever Maureen wrote, it isn't true. We're doing just fine."

"Maureen didn't write me." Harry held a letter just out of her reach. "However, I've been getting an unexplained rash of parking tickets lately. You don't think she's had something to do with it, do you?"

Frowning, Kate reached for the letter, but Harry snatched it away. "If it's not Maureen, then who is the letter from?"

"Jane. Your daughter."

Kate sucked in a deep breath of air so cold it made her eyes water. "I know Jane is my daughter." She stepped closer to Harry. "Why in the world would Jane hire you?"

"It seems that she's inherited the same tendency as her mother to look after people."

His eyes had softened, changed to an expression that set her heart pounding and the strength draining from her limbs.

"What did her friends do?"

"They're going around kissing boys who can't outrun them."

"Kissing boys?" Kate shook her head in disbelief. "Ten-year-old girls?"

"Yep. Every one of them is in detention until Christmas, including Jane."

"Jane? I thought she needed extra help in math and had to take the late bus." She bit her lip thoughtfully. "The little dickens must have forged my signature on a school note."

Each second lightened the darkness around them.

Beyond Harry, the limbs of the old oak tree became
visible. It's thick, dark limbs reached for a mauve-
colored sky. Kate watched without seeing. *Jane's lied
to me?* Her gaze returned to Harry. "How did you get
into all this?"

Harry motioned to the letter in his hand. "I sort of
mentioned if Jane had problems getting into her club,
I'd help her out."

"Club?" Kate's eyes narrowed. "What club?"

The corners of Harry's mouth curved but his voice
stayed solemn. "The kissing boys club. You have to
kiss a boy to get into it."

Jane kissing boys? The image of Jane wearing
shorts in October, and of taping the paperclip to her
navel played through Kate's mind. She couldn't believe that she had missed all the signals that something
major had been going on in Jane's life. She ran a hand
through her hair. "Jane isn't interested in boys."

"Jane wants to be in the club," Harry said in a gentle
voice. "Jane is growing up."

"You knew about this before you left."

Harry nodded.

"She told you, but she didn't tell me?" Kate
couldn't keep the hurt from her voice.

"Because I'm her lawyer."

Her chin came up. "You should have told me."

"I tried, remember? We were standing just about in
this same place."

Suddenly she understood Harry's return. "Now you
feel responsible." She would have winced at her hard,
angry tone if she hadn't been so sure she was right.
"Has it occurred to you coming back here might make
it worse for Jane?" She didn't let him answer. "You're
going to dazzle her with your great legal prowess.

She's going to start counting on you to bail her out, and forget you have another life in Boston. She's going to be devastated when you leave again."

"Are we talking about Jane or are you talking about you?"

"Jane, of course. I know all about men like you. You stick around only when it suits you." Her hands clenched at her sides. "We don't need you or your legal help."

Harry's eyes darkened with anger. He stepped closer until his toes nearly touched the tips of her boots. "Let's get one thing straight, I'm not Roddy."

"Could have fooled me."

"I'm not him." Harry's voice deepened to a growl, and his hands gripped the arms of her thick down jacket.

"The biggest difference is the speed you left." Kate didn't entirely believe her words but said them anyway. "He went about ten miles-per-hour faster." *Does he know my legs are shaking? Does he know how much his leaving hurt?*

"The difference is I came back," Harry replied. "And I'm staying."

"For how long?" Her lips pressed together to keep them from trembling.

"Until forever." Harry pulled her rigid body against his chest. "Want to know how crazy I am? Every one of those parking tickets seemed like a love letter from you."

Her head rested against his chest as the steady pressure of his hands locked behind her back. Kate wanted to believe him, yet didn't. If he felt this way, why hadn't he told her before?

"How many parking tickets did you get?"

"At least thirty."

"Why didn't you change your parking place?"

"I wasn't parked illegally," Harry explained, "and they weren't real tickets. Just one of Maureen's friends doing her a favor. Don't you understand? I wanted some sort of sign that you missed me."

"Missed you?" Kate scoffed. "You burned rubber out of the courthouse lot and didn't even circle the block once."

"If I'd circled, I never would have left." Harry stroked her hair. "I'd made a commitment." He kissed the top of her head. "Besides, I needed to see if what we had was real, or if I'd dreamed the whole thing up."

"And did you?" Kate held her breath.

"Kate, from the moment you hurdled the golf course fence in those tight jeans, you've made my heart race." His eyes shone with the power of his convictions. "The only future I want is the one I share with you." He turned her shoulders to face the Dutch doors and brightening sky. "Let's find out all there is between us."

"I don't know, Harry. You mean it now, but what about later when everything isn't so new?"

"Everything is a risk, Kate. You have to decide if it's worth taking." He looked deeply into her eyes. "The biggest risk for me is losing you. I know what my life was like before you."

Kate looked away from the determination in his eyes. She knew what *he* wanted, but what did *she* want? Behind him, the limbs of the oak tree, bare of leaves, stretched toward her in a silent reminder of her childhood. The rope swing hung from a nearby branch.

"What are you asking, Harry?"

"Your permission to start up my own practice here."

"Here?"

"Anywhere you are."

"But what about your family?"

"What about 'em?"

Kate frowned. "You told them about us?"

"You bet."

Her eyebrows lifted in surprise. "What about your dad's firm?"

"Dad's old friend wanted it. Dad's here," he touched his heart, "not in any building." His gaze bore into hers. "He would have wanted me to make my own way, follow my own dreams. I want a life with you."

Kate studied his face. He looked serious. "I couldn't ask you to do that."

"I'm the one doing the asking." Harry took her hands. "Will you take a chance on us?"

Kate searched his gaze. Her answer would change the lives of so many. "Are you really coming back for me, or for my mother's double chocolate chip brownies?"

"Well, your mother's brownies are good, but not that good."

Her gaze returned to the swing, still strong and sturdy thanks to her dad's care. She and Maureen had spent so many happy hours swinging out of the loft, and then dropping into the hay beneath. She wondered about the girl she had been, and if there were still something of her left inside.

It still seemed too soon to say it was love she felt for Harry. At the same time, her emotions seemed so strong. Seeing him in front of her felt like a gift from God.

Harry didn't comment when she pulled her hands

away. A small furrow appeared between his brows as she strained out the window for the rope swing. Her fingers closed around the fat knot at the bottom. For a moment she held the rope, remembering the very first time she'd gotten up her nerve to swing from it. She pulled the rope, knowing she wasn't testing its strength as much as her own. Was she willing to risk her heart again?

She gazed into Harry's eyes and smiled. "I'm ready to take the chance with you."

A lifetime of promises seemed to pass between them. The rope strained taut as Kate straddled the knot and Harry settled behind her. Taking a deep breath, Kate pushed off. She heard herself laughing as they swung out of the hayloft window.

Epilogue

On the ten-foot ladder, Kate stood with paintbrush
in hand, finishing off the lettering on the sign that
hung from newly oiled chains in the riding academy's
parking lot.

The new sign was only one of the many changes
that had occurred in the past year. The media had
picked up the courtroom story and the resulting pub-
licity had generated new students and boarders.

Kate had financed the repairs to the fence, and faced
no further legal action. She hadn't seen Simon in
months. Rumor had it that he had moved to Florida
and lived on the side of a golf course that did not
adjoin a riding academy. With a new owner, relationships between the two businesses had improved. Kate
didn't complain about the golf balls that frequently
bounced into her riding arena, and no one complained
when the Guinea hens wandered onto the fairway.

Jeb had settled his dispute with the bar association.
The experience had given him such a boost of confi-
dence that he had decided to put off retirement for a

few more years, and help build Harry's new practice.

A few strokes later, Kate regarded the lettering on the new sign. The black lettering stood out clearly: WITHERS' RIDING ACADEMY and underneath BOND & WITHERS, ATTORNEYS AT LAW.

"Are you almost finished up there yet?"

Kate glanced down at Harry, who braced the ladder. She couldn't resist a teasing smile. "Only about an hour more or so," she said sweetly, knowing even if it took all day, Harry wouldn't take a hand off the ladder. Since their marriage six months ago, he had astonished Kate with his thoughtfulness and desire to please her.

She looked down at his chestnut hair gleaming in the summer sun. On her wedding day, Prissy had said, "Everyone always thinks of the wedding day as being the highlight of the relationship, but Kate dear, in a good marriage, the relationship just gets better."

She hoped this was true, both for herself and for Maureen, who had married Jimmy in a joint ceremony.

Kate moved down two steps on the ladder and laughed as Harry grabbed her ankles. "You better let go of me, or I'm going to draw a big heart around your sign. I don't think people will think you're a serious lawyer that way."

He just tightened his grip. Kate checked the sign one last time. To her satisfaction, every letter looked perfectly in place. Apparently, her ineptitude with tools didn't extend to painting.

Harry's new law office, constructed near the spot where the old lean-to had stood, gleamed the same tomato-red color as the barn. She remembered with pride, the first morning they had opened it. The phone had rung immediately, and even if it had only been

Maureen congratulating them, the next calls had been clients. Harry and Jeb had been busy ever since. Jane continued to demonstrate her affinity for law, and spent many an afternoon hanging about the office, or drumming up legal business among the junior riders.

"Looks good." Harry's hand stayed on her until Kate's feet touched the ground. "Especially the paint on your nose."

"I want everything to be perfect for your mother's visit." She rubbed the spot, which smeared immediately.

Harry kissed the tip of her nose. Although Roddy continued to remain distant, his mother finally had replied to the letters and numerous invitations both Kate and Jane had sent.

"Don't worry," Harry said, "she's excited about coming. She reads all of Jane's letters to her friends." He grinned up at her. "They all think Jane has quite a vivid imagination and is going to be the world's next greatest novelist."

Kate returned his grin. "What's your mother going to do when she finds out everything Jane wrote about is true?"

Turning, Harry pointed to the parking lot. "Looks like we're about to find out." He took her hand. "Come on, we'd better go rescue her from the Guinea hens."

Kate looked up at the love and amusement in her husband's eyes. *Of all Your blessings, Lord, thank you for Harry.* With the volume of human and Guinea hen screams steadily increasing, Kate ran toward the surrounded Lincoln Continental.